HUNGER & CURSED SHADOWS

JESSACA WILLIS

HUNGER & CURSED SHADOWS

JESSACA WILLIS

Hunger & Cursed Shadows.

Copyright © 2022 by Jessaca Willis

ISBN: 978-1-953072-06-1

ASIN: B09SPH1L26

All rights reserved. No part of this publication may be reproduced, distributed, or transmitted in any form or by any means, including photocopying, recording, or other electronic or mechanical methods, without the prior written permission of the publisher, except in the case of brief quotations embodied in critical reviews and certain other noncommercial uses permitted by copyright law. For permission requests, write to the publisher, addressed "Attention: Permissions Request," at the address below.

Any reference to historical events, real people, or real places are used fictitiously. Names, characters, and places are products of the author's imagination.

Front cover art by Dark Imaginarium Art Design
Editing by Kate Anderson.

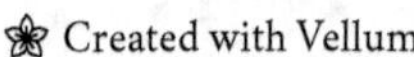 Created with Vellum

BOOKS IN SERIES

PRIMORDIALS OF SHADOWTHORN

Shadow Crusade, Book 1

Blighted Heart, Book 2

Immortal Return, Book 3

BLOOD & MAGIC ETERNAL

Hunger & Cursed Shadows, Book 0

Blood & Magic Eternal, Book 1

Death & Wicked Monsters, Book 2

KALLI

Something dark descends upon the day. I can feel it like a cold, heavy hand clawing at my chest.

But I can't tell a soul.

My sister, Halira, would tell me I'm simply being paranoid. She'd say that after we spent so much of our young lives watching over our shoulders, waiting to run from the demons that bled out of the Shadowthorn snarling and ravenous, that it's to be expected that we would live in constant fear of something terrible interrupting our newly peaceful lives. Our brother, Tor, would say that I'd feel better if I allowed him to train me, and that part of what I fear is being incapable of protecting myself against any of the threats that might arise in our new world. The Elders are least helpful of all, for in their sage wisdom, they'd remind me that wounds of the mind and heart such as the ones we harbor can sometimes take years to heal, even decades. They'd advise me to inhale the fresh scent of the forest to clear away any dark cloud that should pass me by.

But what am I to do when I inhale and all I breathe in is death?

Something is wrong today.

Despite the shining sun, there's a dark shadow filtering through the trees, reminding me of the days of the Shadowthorn, when the blighted forest encroached too close and shrouded our hometown in misery.

As an Elder myself now, people turn to me for answers.

For comfort.

For protection.

What if I can't provide it?

"Hello?" My sister draws out the last syllable, her hand waving before me. "Kalli? Are you even listening?"

"Hmm?"

I snap out of my fugue to find myself in the middle of the treetop market. All around us, the people of the Eyve are exuberant, joyous. It's been so long since they've had the freedom to leave their homeland, and thanks to Halira, my impossibly hopeful, brave, and reckless younger sister, they can now leave the safety of the village and see the world.

But why would any of them ever leave when they feel so much serenity and joy here?

Everywhere I turn, I'm reminded of just how vastly different the Eyve is from Gravenburg, where we grew up. The dreary, stone buildings that looked like they were on the brink of collapsing are replaced by natural woods and verdant foliage. The dark clouds that had dimmed our skies are nowhere in sight, the sun beaming cheerily upon us as if it shines for these people, and these people alone.

But it's the magic that truly brings this place to life.

Just ahead of us, two sparrows fly around, caught in a cute game of chase as they weave in and out of the heads of the people. They finally dive for the ground, but before they crash, their feathers shift, noses replacing beaks, and soon there are two boisterous men—perhaps brothers—standing in their place. Beside them, one of the vendors, an older woman with skin as wrinkled as fruit left to ripen in the sun and eyes as bright as stars, speaks to the plants on her table, making their vines dance and wave in response. Some of the people here speak to the squirrels, others have set up shop to heal an assortment of ailments with nothing more than incantations and the soft touch of their hands.

Like I had to do when we fought the Primordial.

This time when I don't answer, Halira snaps her fingers, nearly catching the tip of my nose. "Seriously, Kalli, you're scaring me. Where are you today?"

I shake my head, but she won't drop it. She folds her arms, looking every inch the spitting image of our mother, even though I'm usually the one who that ghost haunts.

"You can't lie to me. I just told you I was"—she lowers her voice, despite the loudness of the marketplace, ensuring that no one will be able to hear her—"pregnant."

"You're what?" My eyes bulge, hearing her for the first time.

She throws her arms up. "See? This is what I'm saying."

"I'm sorry. Excuse me for being surprised when my younger sister abruptly announces that she's preg—" She glares at my volume, and out of respect, I oblige, dropping my tone an octave and leaning in closer. "You're really pregnant?"

"That's what I was saying, yes."

I cross my arms. "Well, I'm sorry I didn't hear you. I must've had something else on my mind."

"It's been difficult not to notice. You've been distracted all morning. What's going on with you today?"

I press my lips together. I hadn't wanted to tell her. Isn't the whole point of being an older sister to shield the other from anything that might hurt her? She's had so much on her plate these past few months. She singlehandedly destroyed the Blight that had infested these lands for genera-tions. She freed the Primordial from her dark imprisonment, along with many other druids—including our own brother.

She defeated the mages and restored magic to its natural balance. The last thing I want is to put more responsibility on her. Especially when I'm not even sure what has me on edge. A feeling? That's hardly enough reason to rouse her suspicions.

She's earned the rest. I should keep my *feelings* to myself.

But I can tell she's not going to drop it.

I meander through the crowd, stopping only to glance at a table of clay necklaces, one of them catching my eye. As I pick up the bee-shaped bead that reminds me of my mother, Halira appears beside me. She must not see what I'm holding, or maybe she can't be distracted by thoughts of our mother today, because she yanks the necklace away and tosses it back onto the stand.

"Wrong how?" she presses me. "Talk to me. You don't have to keep everything so...so bottled in."

Whipping around, I meet her apologetic eyes with a fiery glare. "I don't know! Okay? This is why I didn't say anything. I hardly have anything concrete to share. It just feels like something is wrong. That's all."

Halira watches me thoughtfully, both of us doing our best to ignore the worried glances we're accumulating from everyone within earshot. While she thinks, her hand starts to float, perhaps of its own accord, to her belly. To think I could be an auntie someday. The thought had truly never crossed my mind. Before we defeated the mages and united the realms, I had been so focused on my career at the Capital that the idea of the Devonshire family growing had been the farthest thought from my mind. Maybe even less so once our older brother, Tor, disappeared in the Shadowthorn, presumed dead for several years.

I mourn for our parents not being able to see us now. They died believing Tor dead. They died thinking Halira would spend her years tending to our family beehives, and that I'd have a successful career as a member of the Magistrate's Senate.

Oh, how vastly different things have come to be since then.

Halira must realize where her hand is drifting, and more importantly that we're out in public and people are still casting wary eyes upon us, because she jerks her hand away and tidies the black Crusader tunic she still insists on wearing.

"Should I tell Ryven?"

My face heats. "Tell Ryven what? That I'm being crazy?"

"Piss on a mage, Kalli. Try to stay focused. I'm not talking about your paranoia. I'm talking about the baby!"

Shame stings me like a hundred of our mother's bees. What is wrong with me today? My inability to maintain focus today is unacceptable. I'm an Elder, for crying out loud. I shouldn't be so easily distracted by worries. Halira has every right to be frustrated with me.

"I'm sorry. I—I don't know. That's your choice to make. Not mine."

Halira gives me a look that suggests she's just about had enough of me today.

Before either of us can try to save the interaction from the disaster I've made of it, someone calls from behind us.

"Elder Kalli!"

Twisting toward the smoky voice, I find a cloaked woman with raven hair pushing through the crowd. Silver was one of the few former Crusaders to remain in the Eyve once the battle with the mages ended. For whatever reason, she and Güthric—who marches beside her now and helps with clearing their path—said this place just felt like home. I have a feeling that it had more to do with wanting to stay near Halira and Ryven though, two of the only friends who survived the ordeal.

Last I heard, they were spending some time in Heartkeep for their honeymoon.

Their being here only serves to strangle the knots that have been tied in my belly all morning. Any second now, the sky will soon fall.

"What are you two doing here?" Halira asks, frowning. The dark shadow that creases her forehead reminds me of the necroink she and the other Crusaders used to wear to protect themselves from the fiends of the Shadowthorn. If only her scowling could protect us from whatever it is they've come to tell us. "I thought you weren't due back for another week?"

"We weren't," Silver says, her voice like a peaceful, ethereal breeze.

Güthric's is the opposite, all mountainous echoes and rumbling earthquakes. "Trouble."

My sister turns to me, trepidation and apology warring in her expression.

"Not here," I tell the three of them. Whatever the information they have for us, it's most certainly the reason I've been on edge all day. I don't know how I know it, but I know we need to speak in private. "Come. We can speak in our aunt's home. It's not far."

After a short, brisk walk, hastened by Halira's manipulation of the wind at our feet, we find our Aunt Imryll's home empty. The door has barely closed behind us before Silver can no longer bite her tongue.

"They've come back."

I fear I already know who the *they* is that she's referring to, but I have to ask.

"Who's *they*?"

She stands taller, Güthric's hand squeezed tightly in hers. "The demons. They just attacked Heartkeep."

2

KALLI

"That's—that can't be." Halira paces the room, shaking her head furiously. She turns her pleading eyes on me. "We got rid of them. I know we did. We spent months making sure..."

Outside, the wind howls, Halira's frantic state like puppet strings to the dark clouds that roll in overhead. If anyone has the right to be panicking at the thought of having to face demonkind again, it's her. After all, she's already suffered so much to ensure that no one else had to face demons again.

The wooden walls of our aunt's abode do little to conceal the concerned murmurs outside. It's upsetting enough when a beautiful, bright day takes a turn so suddenly, but they know better than to presume the darkening of the sky is anything but magical.

I want to offer her an embrace. Or at least, I feel like that's something people would do in this scenario. But the thought makes my skin feel like it's strangling my own bones.

If Ryven were here, he'd know how to give her the comfort she needs, and therefore soothe the worrying people outside by making the storm dissipate.

Without him present, I can only rely on my own skills, what I'm good at: logic.

"Halira's correct. The Shadowthorn was destroyed. The Primordial was saved and in doing so, demonkind was eradicated months ago. It's why druids like Tor who had been trapped in demon flesh were released from their prisons. The Blight is over. Demons are a thing of the past."

The window stops rattling, the wind subsiding and returning to a more natural breeze.

Güthric shakes his head, blond hair sweeping his broad shoulders. With the hand not laced with Silver's, he reaches for his heart, claws digging into his chest as he pantomimes the grotesque nature of their report. "Demons killed."

My jaw tightens. "How can you be sure? Did you see it?"

"No, it was gone by the time we were summoned, but we saw the poor woman. She was undoubtedly bitten," Silver says firmly. "The bite wasn't as severe as it could've been, thankfully. We'll be able to talk to her once she awakens, but no other creature could've done it—"

"Wait." Halira's head jerks up, fear turning her gaze dark and ashy. "She's still alive?"

Silver nods.

"That's not possible," I say, glancing between the three of them. My knowledge of demonkind is limited only to what I witnessed growing up near the Shadowthorn border and what I heard from the tales that spread through the villages. But one thing that's always been true is no one survives a demon bite.

At least, they hadn't until we discovered druids.

"She's a druid then?" I ask them.

But Silver suddenly looks like she's in pain. "We didn't think so. According to the family, there is no sign of magic throughout their lineage. But she has to be to have survived this long."

Halira finally stills from her pacing, only to pull at one of her strands of white hair and starts curling it around her finger. "What did the bite look like?"

Silver gives her shoulders a bob. "I don't know. Like a bite. You can see where the fangs—"

The door bursts open before she can finish her description, a fluttering of black wings whizzing past us all to envelop Halira in a leathery blanket. In the blink of an eye, the large bat shifts into a man with dark hair and darker eyes. No horns though. Not anymore. Not ever since he was cured of the Blight. Sometimes I still expect to see them, especially whenever he takes on his shadowbat form.

"Are you alright?" Ryven asks, checking Halira over and frowning at the sight of her nervous hands. "I saw the clouds and felt the wind. What's going on?"

Biting her lip, all my sister can do is look up at him, her big eyes pleading. I can only imagine how difficult this news must be for her, someone who fought so hard so that she'd never have to face demonkind again. But I think we both fear how much more difficult it will be for Ryven, someone who had been bitten by a demon, survived the blighted poison, only to then turn into one of the vile creatures and lose almost all his autonomy.

After a stretched moment, Halira throws herself into his arms, and he glances between the three of us.

"What happened in Heartkeep?" He must deduce this from the unexpected presence of his friends.

"Demons," Güthric answers.

Ryven's sun-kissed complexion falls ashen, but he holds onto a healthy amount of skepticism as he beseeches Halira. "Is this true?"

"We don't know for certain," I say, trying to appease both of their nerves—and perhaps my own, as well. "We have no proof."

"We saw her body," Silver insists, irritation edging her words. "What more proof do you need?"

I don't have an answer for her. The truth is, it is unlikely that there is any amount of proof that would convince me she's right because I rely on logic, and the logic of it all just doesn't add up. Demons only existed because the magic waters of Bagamore were being pilfered by greedy mages. But we put an end to their meddling and now the Pits of Bagamore are safely guarded at all times. The Primordial herself is benevolent and pristine. There is simply no possible way for demons to exist without her doing, and she has no reason to create them anymore.

I would argue with Silver all day and night if it took that long to convince her that she's mistaken. Perhaps the woman in Heartkeep was bitten by a bear or some other beast instead?

Fortunately for everyone, Ryven saves us the time with his excellent suggestion.

"The only proof I need is seeing it with my own eyes."

* * *

No one argues the suggestion. We leave for Heartkeep immediately.

On our way out of the Eyve, I realize I haven't informed the other Elders that I'll be away, so Halira sends a whisper on the wind to them on my behalf. The reply she receives is one of caution, the Elders advising us to tread carefully because the trees have been restless of late. It doesn't make me feel any better.

We arrive at Heartkeep a few hours later, before the sun has fully begun its descent over the horizon.

"This way." Silver guides us through the quiet town. Heartkeep is one of the United Realm's newest villages, established just a few short months ago after the fall of the Shadowthorn. The town rests where the Primordial Qaeus' heart had slumbered before Halira awoke the being, hence the name *Heartkeep*. The village itself is far from completion, growing each and every day as more structures and homes are built. The goal is for Heartkeep to become another of the main cities, like Gravenburg, but only time will tell if people will flock to this historical corner of the realm.

Especially if rumors of demons leak from it.

Silver knocks on a wooden door and we're beckoned inside the home of a woman with a bowl of something goopy on her hip and a brood of children nipping about her ankles. With minimal conversation, she takes us into the back room where her sister rests. Only the poor girl is hardly recognizable as her younger sister anymore. She looks more like something that's been dead for a few months than anything human and living. But even from the doorway, I can see the rapid rise and fall of her chest.

"How long ago was she bitten?" I ask Silver as Halira and Ryven shove into the room.

"Earlier this morning," she says, utterly flabbergasted. "She didn't look like this when we left."

I join Halira and Ryven beside the woman. Güthric and Silver remain in the doorway, allowing the three of us space to examine her wounds—or perhaps, I realize, they're guarding the door in case the demon returns to finish what it's started.

Her pulse is rapid, and her breathing is shallow. A sheen of sweat glistens over her sickly ashen forehead. Otherwise, she appears surprisingly well for someone who's just been bitten by a demon.

Halira is the one to tug the woman's collar down, two strange pinpricks revealing themselves on her neck.

It's unlike the carnage I remember seeing when our home

was attacked. Those creatures devoured on our neighbors like dogs gnawing on bones. The wounds we saw then were gaping, entire sections of people's bodies gouged out and swallowed. The amount of viscera that covered the streets was staggering, even days later when I arrived.

Our own parents weren't even whole when we set them on the pyres and released their spirits to the gods.

The holes in this woman are careful by comparison.

Clean.

Precise.

Effective.

"Is this the only bite?" Halira asks over her shoulder.

Silver and Güthric nod.

"It's not a demon bite," Ryven argues. Leaning in close to get a better look, he angles his nose at them and sniffs, but pulls back embarrassed. Even months after becoming human again, he's still adjusting to the loss of some of the instincts he'd developed when he was a demon.

It's my turn to get a better look at the woman.

"Whatever bit into her wasn't doing so to eat her flesh." Delicately, I trace the two, circular wounds, the skin hard but tacky from the dried blood. "It reminds me of a snake bite. Or a spider."

Güthric grunts. "Big spider."

My sister ignores him, and I'm grateful that she's able to focus on the correct piece of information I'm mulling over.

"You think the bite was just meant to poison her? But why?"

"I don't know," I answer, unable to peel my eyes away from the wounds. Inwardly, my mind is fast at work. What do we know about snakes and spiders? And what similarities do we see with this woman? "Spiders inject poison but it's not actually what kills them. They use it to immobilize their prey long enough to eat them."

Behind us, Silver growls her frustration. "Now we're saying a human-eating spider came after her?"

"I've seen stranger things," Ryven says, sharing a private, knowing look with Halira.

"I really don't want to have to kill another giant spider."

"Hopefully it doesn't come down to that," I say. "I'm merely making connections. Hypothesizing."

This was the part of my old profession that I loved. The mental work it took to determine which policies would best suit the nation, how to handle conflicts between lords, or managing armies, materials, and other supplies, it was the math my mind craved. And it's an aspect of my current role that I don't get to enjoy often.

My gaze drifts to the woman's gaunt and pale face. "She's lost a lot of blood, but I see no signs of it on her clothes. There aren't even streaks down her neck. Whatever bit her—and I'm not saying it was a spider, only that it acts like one—whatever it was, it fed on her blood. I'm almost certain."

I can feel the tension in the room expand, the weight of it pressing into every one of us.

Silver prepares to defend her argument again, to tell us for dozenth time why this...this *thing* has to be a demon. As much as I'd love to believe her, the facts just aren't adding up. Arcathainians are well-versed with demon bites. She should be too, being a former Crusader. But I suppose it's easier to face something you're familiar with than an unknown threat.

A wheeze smothers the silence. It carries into the air like a cloud of dust rising from an ancient, forgotten tome. It fills the room like death.

I'm not the only one whose breath catches in their lungs as I turn my attention back to the woman. To her ribcage.

Her lungs are still. They don't fill with any other breath.

Just to be sure, Ryven checks her pulse, but all he does is confirm what we already know.

The woman is dead.

The others stare mournfully at her corpse, guilt etched in all of their faces. I want to grab Halira's shoulders and shake her. How long will it take for her to realize she can't save them all? How long before the rest of them realize that there will always be lives lost to battle?

This was never about saving this woman. She was as good as dead by the time we arrived—earlier, even, given her injuries and the speed with which this single bite defeated her. Her demise was kissed upon her neck like a promise earlier this morning.

No, this wasn't about the woman. This was about preparing for what comes next.

Without warning, the screech of a dying gull belches from the dead woman's lungs. She bursts upright on her bed. Halira, Ryven, and I stumble backward; we don't stop until our backs are slammed up against the wall.

The woman, bony and grey, gasps horrifically, as she claws at nothing and anything. She tears at the bedsheets tucked firmly around her body; her bloodshot eyes fixed on us like we're to blame.

My heart hammers in my throat. "Wh-what do we do?"

I look to the four people around me. Together, they've faced droves of demons, they've battled mages. They're far more experienced in these matters than I.

"Why are you asking us?" Silver snaps, her back pressed against the door. "Aren't you the healer?"

Incredulously, I gawk at the reanimated woman. She hangs from the edge of her bed and thrashes, reminding me of seaweed flailing in a strong current, only if seaweed had razor-sharp fangs. Where did those come from? And when?

"She doesn't need a healer. She needs a sword."

Halira charges forward, her sneering face mere inches from mine. "Everyone said the same about Ryven. They said I should just put him out of his misery because he couldn't be cured, but I found a way."

Behind her, just out of the corner of my eye, I notice something unreadable darken Ryven's expression. By the time I can focus my attention on him, it's gone.

I open my mouth to explain our current predicament in as simple of terms as I can manage, when the previously-dead woman finally falls from her bed, landing head-first.

Her skull cracks. Blood seeps from her sweaty hair. But the girl keeps moving. Keeps clawing. Keeps snarling.

A shiver slides down my spine when she begins dragging her body, legs still tangled in the blankets, across the floor. Saliva dribbles from her mouth as she chomps at us.

I might not have as much experience battling demons as the rest of them, but I recognize the look of hunger in a wild beast's eyes.

"Look at her!" I scream. "She means to kill us! Someone do something!"

No one moves.

"We can try speaking to her," Ryven suggests to Halira. "The way you spoke to me when I was still blighted."

"That won't work—"

I interrupt my sister before she can tell us why. She'd be giving the wrong answer anyway. "Of course it won't."

Before anyone can stop me, I reach around my sister and pull out Ryven's sword. It's even heavier than I estimated it would be, given the decorative hilt and the broad blade, but I use my awkward stumbling to my advantage.

"No!"

With my staggering momentum, I aim the sword, and shove it through the ghoulish creature's face. Some might lament over what they've done—I know Halira would. But I know better. This woman died this morning, not here by my hands.

I toss the sword to the ground.

"There. Now can we please focus on what's important here?" Halira scoffs, the look in her eyes one of utter disbelief. I ignore it. "This woman was bitten by something that was delicate and quiet. It took care making the incisions on her neck and it showed restraint in drinking her blood—it left enough in her that she was still alive."

Bending down, I grab the back of the woman's head and lift her up. Since most of my sword went through her eye and nose, her jaw is largely intact, and I gesture to the infinite-seeming number of serrated teeth in her maw.

"This creature couldn't have left those marks. And I can promise you that she would've been vicious in her kill. If she had gotten ahold of us, it would've been a bloodbath."

Tears stream down Halira's cheeks. "You don't know that—"

"I do! And so would you if you'd start thinking with your head instead of letting your..."

I almost spill her secret. I almost blame Halira's sensitive heart on the baby she's carrying in her womb. But that wouldn't be fair, and it wouldn't be accurate. Halira has always cared deeply about everyone. I can understand her sympathy, but I have no patience for the way it's impeding our ability to get to the bottom of this.

After all, if we can't crack this mystery, more will die.

More might, even if we do.

Sighing, I shift my shoulders and stand taller. "I just want to figure this out so we can stop it from happening again."

Halira wipes at her cheeks.

I open my mouth to continue my line of thinking—I've learned recently that speaking out loud can sometimes help.

A commotion bangs in the other room. Our heads spin. Frantic footsteps thud into the main room.

Through the boards of the walls, we hear a stranger shout, "We got 'im! We caught the blighted prick that attacked your sister."

The five of us barrel into the room before the sister can even utter her appreciation, unaware that her grief has only just begun.

"Where?" Halira asks the man.

I do her one better. "Take us to him."

HALIRA

My eyes still burn as the pot-bellied stranger leads us outside, the crisp night air not helping. With Ryven's arm draped across my shoulder, the ache in my heart only worsens. That could've been him. He could've died at the hands of someone who didn't believe in saving him. Piss on a mage! That could've been our brother if any Crusader had come across him during his time as one of the behemoths.

I can't even look at Kalli. She's always been cold. She's always chosen the path of reason over one of emotion. But this?

She just killed a woman, and yet she's striding through this town with her head held high.

I don't know whether to envy her, pity her, or be worried.

"It's alright," Ryven says into my hair before planting a kiss on the top of my head. "Your sister's just trying to do what she thinks is right."

My head jerks up. "And you agree with her?"

"I didn't say that." His brown eyes are soft. All the comfort I ever need can be found inside their embrace and I allow myself to fall into them. "I just mean that...whatever's going on, it's not good. And you might not agree with Kalli on everything, but in times like these, it's good to have family. You'll need her in the days to come."

I smile up at the man that will soon be a father and think about how lucky I am to have him—how lucky we both are. If he hadn't stopped his friend, Ahl'Ro, who'd been trapped in a demon's skin and lost in a murderous rampage through Gravenburg, I'd be dead. If I hadn't selected the Primordial axe from among the dozens of weapons presented to the Crusader initiates, we wouldn't have been able to free the Primordial Qaeus, cross the Varenholm Ocean, and reach the Pits of Bagamore where he was cured of the Blight.

Since the beginning, he's always looked out for me. Some things, I guess, never change.

"Thank you," I mouth to him as the round man stops before a barn.

"He's in there," he says, gesturing to the great wooden doors like they're covered in carnivorous vines.

But truthfully, this barn is about the cleanest I've ever laid eyes on. Much of the buildings in Heartkeep are. It makes me happy for the people who will live here. Growing up in the Wallows, I'd just assumed it was normal for every roof to leak, every floorboard to flood when it rains. The people who live here will be able to build a good life for themselves.

Assuming we can put an end to whatever monster has found itself at their doorsteps.

The man leaves us, scrambling to get as far away from the barn as he can before we open it. Güthric walks forward, but I'm not willing to let him—or any of the people I care about, for that matter—walk into danger blindly. After all, what's the point of having magic if you can't use it to protect the ones you love?

A gale of wind races from every direction, gaining speed until it reaches us and blasts through the wooden doors. They bang as they swing ajar, my wind holding them open and creating a path for the rest of us to enter.

Güthric and Ryven enter first, with me, Silver, and Kalli close behind. I'm taking the place in when the men stop abruptly.

"No," Ryven breathes, his voice cracking.

"What?" I ask, shoving past him, somehow already knowing that the reason for his pain is because he knows whatever we've just stumbled upon will hurt me.

He's not wrong.

I gasp at the sight of the man sitting on the ground, arms bound behind his back to a pole. Though I can't see his face, the long, white hair covering it is unmistakable.

"Tor?" My voice wavers. I crash to my knees beside him and force him to look at me. "What are you—"

This time I'm not the only one to gasp. Kalli has found her way to the front of the group and can finally see him as well. The blood crusted on his lips makes for a slightly more shocking sight though, and she is less inclined to collapse beside him, or go anywhere near him, for that matter.

"I don't understand," I say, peering up to the rest of them. Thanks to the events of earlier, my eyes are already primed to release whatever emotions I need to let flow. Hopefully I don't spend my entire pregnancy so emotionally vulnerable.

Something awful and unlike anything I've ever seen from him contorts his expression.

"What are you doing here?" he asks, voice hoarse.

Perhaps afraid of the answer any of them will provide, I turn back to him. "I could ask you the same."

When Tor was first cured of the Blight, the first time I gazed into his eyes after he'd returned to his human self, I swore that I could see every kill he'd made as a demon. For years he was trapped in that form. Not like Ryven, who maintained some of his consciousness—a fate that I'm still not sure was better or worse—but at least he wasn't *gone*, not in the way that Tor was. Ryven hadn't succumbed to the animal inside him. Inside us all.

When I looked into Tor's eyes that day, I saw death, but I also saw his shame.

I see the same thing now.

"Heartkeep reported an attack. A woman was bitten. They believed it to be a demon, but the signs are incongruous."

Kalli sounds as if she's in the middle of one of her Senate hearings. She might as well be reading a report to our heartless Uncle Esmond, the former and late Magistrate of Arcathain.

"Kalli!" I say, whirling around where I'm crouched. "Stop acting like you're passing judgment on some nobody from a town you've never been to. He's our brother!"

"And I'm an Elder." When she says it, it's not in the conceited way that some might. There's almost a hint of sorrow buried somewhere in those words. "I have people to protect. Laws to uphold."

Scoffing, I scoot around to Tor's back and begin fumbling with the knots.

"Yeah, well, I don't. I have *family* to protect. That's all I care about."

"Halira, don't be—"

"What?" My voice squeaks. "Don't be reasonable? Don't unbound our brother so that we can have a decent, respectable conversation with him? Are you joking right now?" The dead woman's face flashes in my mind. "You just a killed a woman! And you're going to preach to me about upholding laws?"

Tor's interest suddenly piques. "You killed her? Why? Why would you do that?"

"She was dead already. The moment she was bitten, I believe she was infected, or something. We'll need to run some tests. Maybe the druids have magic that can help us—"

"No," he mutters. "She was fine. I know she was fine!"

I finish untying the knot in the same instance I begin to wonder whether my sister was right in wanting to leave it in place. Cautiously, I back away, slinking to Ryven's side and trying to keep my blighted hand away from my belly, from the child I was so happy to bring into this newly untainted world.

Tor rubs at his wrists and thanks me.

"Tell us what you know," Kalli says.

"I will." Our brother nods before running a shaking hand through his hair. "Fuck. I will. I should've told you sooner, but I —I didn't know what was happening. I knew something was wrong but—I didn't understand it. I just—"

"Slow down," Ryven advises, his fingers drawing circles on my shoulder. "Start from the beginning. When did you first notice something was wrong?"

"Ever since I came back," my brother whimpers, and I've never seen him look so broken in my life. "Something's wrong with me... I'm different."

"Different how?" Kalli probes.

He hesitates, wide eyes peering up at us, then to the door, like he's trying to assess whether to run.

A breeze whispers through my fingers and I aim it at his ear. "Don't do that. Whatever you did, whatever you're afraid of, we want to help you. Or at least, I do. You know how Kalli is."

The smirk that twitches his mouth makes my heart sing. At least I know I can still reach him, no matter what he's going through. Family is what I care about.

He inhales deeply, his chest shuddering. "Different...in that, my appetite has changed."

Silence settles. No one needs to ask him what he means. A woman had her neck bitten and her blood drained. Our vivid imaginations can fill in the rest.

Kalli snaps her attention to Ryven and I. "What about you two?"

"What?" I'm stunned into incoherence for a moment until I can gather my thoughts. "You've gone mad. You can't just go around accusing people like that."

"I can, and I am. Answer the question."

My mouth hangs agape. "What makes you think that something's different with Ryven and I?"

"The Blight," she says simply. "I'm curious if that is a factor here. Tor was blighted. For three years he was a demon and fed upon flesh. Now he's human and still craving it."

"Blood," he corrects.

She waves him off. "I want to know if there's a pattern because if there is then we have a bigger problem on our hands."

With sinking dread, I realize she's right. There's no telling how many druids were freed from their demonic prisons when the Pits of Bagamore were cleansed. A few dozen at least? Maybe more? It's not nearly as devastating as the horde of demons that lived in the Shadowthorn were, but considering what their bite seems to do to humans? How it changed that woman? This problem could get bigger, fast.

"No," I finally say. "I'm fine. No...thirst for blood."

"And you?" Kalli turns her sharp attention to Ryven.

"He's been fine, too," I snap, my protectiveness of him still as strong as the day the Blight overcame him. Wrapping my arm around his waist, I tug him closer. "Tell her. "

But when my eyes search for his, he avoids them.

Doubt wriggles into my thoughts.

"Ryven?"

He doesn't have a chance to answer me.

"That settles it." Kalli twists on her heels, moving so fast that the rest of us are left scrambling in her wake. "This problem is bigger than we thought. It's time we spoke with the Elders."

4

HALIRA

It's getting late, and since my sister, my brother, Ryven, and I can all travel much quicker with use of our magic, and since Silver and Güthric had been staying in Heart-keep anyway, they opt to remain behind, on the condition that we send them an update if the Elders have anything else to tell us.

Then, it's to the sky.

Wings and wind.

Ryven takes on the form of a bat, a creature to which he's become rather accustomed. I often wonder how he can even stomach being associated with the same beast he'd been when he was blighted, but I don't dare ask him. If he's alright with it, then so am I.

In her element of night, Kalli flies through the sky as a blur of white, her snow owl just as beautiful and graceful as her.

Even Tor has learned to hone the druid power of shapeshifting, though just like every other time, the shape he takes tonight differs from his last. He looks like a crow, reminding me of our Aunt Imryll, only bigger. His wingspan could be double her size, and his speed is equally impressive.

None of them can match me, though.

I dissipate into air itself and ride my own torrent of wind. I could make it to the Eyve in half the time as the rest of them, but I opt not to. Part of me doesn't want to face the Elders on my own, not when we bring such terrifying news.

Besides, Heartkeep isn't so far from the Eyve that it's much of a journey at all. We reach the border in a third of the time it took us to walk there. And with Kalli leading the way into the Elder tree, I don't feel as though we're intruding upon them, like I have some of the other times I've arrived uninvited.

"You've returned." The Elder Henness, the eldest of the three women huddled among the bookshelves, peers up from her search with vibrant green, knowing eyes. "Your trip was worse than you expected."

Beside her, Elder Irene hugs a small stack of books closer to her chest. "I'm not confident that we can aid you with what you seek."

Grey, silken hair dances at her shoulders in a self-made zephyr. I've learned a lot from her these past few months. Wielding the winds in battle had been a show of strength, not finesse, and Elder Irene has mastered the latter. With her instruction, I've honed my power. I can summon hurricanes just as easily as I can send a secret on a tendril of air meant for one person's ears through a crowd of thousands.

I used that very skill during our return to the Eyve when I sent a message to the Elders updating them on what we found and trying to prepare them for our arrival. We'd asked them to search for any answers that might be hiding in the history books about previous mutations of demons, the Primordials magic, the Pits of Bagamore.

Judging from their defeated expressions, it doesn't look like they've found any. The only one among them who appears to be in good spirits is the third Elder—Elder Nebadri. With the way she anxiously fidgets with the bird perched on her head, it's the most normal I've seen her in a few days, what with the tragedy that befell one of her mice companions. It was near impossible to get her that sometimes even the animals are out of a druid's influence and that sometimes a fox or an owl or a house cat just wants to eat a mouse, regardless of who the creature may belong to.

However, in hindsight, maybe we were wrong to assume it was something as innocuous as a fox who'd torn the creature to pieces...

"Thank you for looking," Kalli says to the Elders, then addresses me. "We should send word to the other towns. Warn them about what is to come."

But it's Elder Henness who replies. "Elder Irene already reached out to the neighboring communities. It's much the same. The attacks on humans, the illness that follows, and the swift death that results in some sort of...horrific second life."

"Not all," Elder Irene adds in her ethereal tone. "Some poor, unfortunate souls made no transformation because they were left for dead. Drained of every last drop of blood."

Panic inches up my throat. "How many? Dead and changed?"

"It's difficult to say," my mentor responds. She lifts a finger, a small cyclone of wind circling around her fingertip. "Here."

With a flick of her finger, she sends it across the cluttered room to me.

I catch it in my palm, the messages from dozens of villagers and townspeople practically screaming as they float up from my hand. Kalli leans in, listening. Tor does as well, the intrigue in his silver eyes concerning.

Ryven is the only one who stands back. He hasn't unfolded his arms since we entered the Elder tree. The concerned furrow of his brow hasn't lessened either, though I'm not sure it has anything to do with what's been said. He's somewhere else entirely.

Lost in thought.

Lost in fear.

I want to reach out to him. I want to squeeze his hand and remind him that he's been through worse and survived. We'll get through this too. We won't let the darkness win.

But he's been known to disappear when the darkness encroaches. When the Blight consumed him and he became that behemoth shadowbat, he fled to spare us. To spare me.

He can't run this time. I can't afford to lose him again. *We* can't afford to lose him.

My thumb strokes my belly as the cyclone dissipates back into the ether. Messages received, Kalli and I exchange a glance.

"Dozens," I breathe, their voices a roar in my head. "There have been dozens already."

"Why are we just now hearing about this?"

Kalli doesn't aim the question at anyone in particular. It's just her audibly mulling-over new information, trying to make sense of it all. But Elder Henness answers her.

"I suspect it's because the humans are distrustful of our kind. They've been told that magic is evil, and even though the magic the mages stole might've been vile and distrusting, they haven't yet come to understand that druid magic can be different."

My sister's fists ball at her sides. "It's foolish! They'd rather die than ask us for help, despite us proving our loyalty to them tenfold! The country wouldn't be whole without us. The Primordial would still be a destructive monster if it wasn't for the magic Halira used to protect Arcathain."

"Give them time," Henness advises. "A centuries-old fear doesn't disappear overnight. It could take generations for that healing to happen, but it will come. Until then, we remain true to ourselves. We keep our people protected."

The insinuation makes my blood boil. "And by our people, we *are* talking about everyone in the United Realm, correct?"

A nearly imperceptible shrug is the only answer Elder Henness gives.

"Of course we are," Kalli says, glaring at the woman. "Even if they don't want our help, we'll still provide it. Halira, can you send a message out to all the villages and towns in the realm?"

"All of them? I-I've never done something of that scale before."

Ryven flashes me a crooked smile. "Says the woman who faced the Primordial and an entire legion of mages."

It's difficult not to blush. "This is different though. Controlling the winds in our surrounding area is one thing, but the farther away I send them, the weaker they become."

"Then send them as far as you can," Kalli instructs, thumb pressed thoughtfully against her lip. "Tell them—"

A throaty rumble vibrates the foundation of the tree before she can finish, the hollowed oak creaking and moaning in pain. Everyone braces themselves, the ground quaking violently beneath us and threatening to knock us off our feet. Books fall from the shelves. The Elders huddle together and stagger toward their sofa for cover, or to at least be away from the death trap of the tall shelves.

I clutch onto Ryven, his sturdy stance all I need to keep me planted in place.

Until a gale of wind thunders through the front door, blasting the thing off its hinges. My sister and brother dive out of the way, but I'm blinded by the raging winds before I can see where they land, if they're alright.

Agony roars into the room.

Something ancient and scared hisses around me, through my hair, and into my ears.

I gasp, the voice unmistakable. Heart wrenching.

The winds stop abruptly, the source of their bellowing cut short.

"It can't be..." I breathe into the quiet of the room.

Weak but regaining strength, Kalli pushes herself up from where she and Tor crashed to the floor. "What? What is it? What did you hear?"

I look to Elder Irene for some help, forgetting that I'm the only one in this room that could've possibly deciphered the message. For I am the only one who can speak with the Primordial Qaeus.

"It's the Primordial..." I say, voice as shaky as my nerves. "She...she just died."

5

TOR

Across the room, the Elders collapse in hysterics. Halira and Kalli blink but there's nothing but numbness reflected in their gazes.

Only Ryven and I have other matters on our minds.

Our secret is out. Not one that we shared knowingly, but the secret we've both been hiding—that apparently *all* the behemoths have been hiding—since the day we found each other in that wasteland, human once more.

For the first week, I'd awaken in a cold sweat, heart racing, teeth chattering from a cold that wasn't in the room with me, but one that had nestled itself around my heart. I was ravaged by memories that weren't mine. Demon claws digging through the intestines of a lost Crusader. Blood filling my mouth until I was almost gagging on it. Screams. Running. Darkness.

Whenever I craved blood, I assumed it was a lingering side effect of the time I'd spent blighted and trapped in a demon's skin, and I certainly wasn't going to bother my sisters with it. They'd taken on the world, and in so doing, saved people like me. I didn't need to burden them with trauma that just needed time to heal.

But even as the dreams became less frequent, the images less severe, the thirst remained.

I wanted blood.

I still do.

And when my eyes find Ryven across the room, cradling my younger sister in his arms as her legs give out, I can tell he wants it too. His square jaw flexes with the restraint it takes not to sink his fangs into her neck. I both appreciate and applaud him for that. Losing Halira is the last thing I want, but I know it's only a matter of time.

The urge is worsening. My ability to keep human food down has become near impossible. The only thing left to do was to give in to the temptation, to feast on the blood that my body had been craving. I thought if I let her live, it would be okay. But if our bites are deadly to them, then I don't know what to do. I need blood just as my sisters need air to breathe.

Forever the image of strength, Kalli is first to recover.

"Halira, send word to the other communities. Do it now. Tell them to find all of the formerly blighted druids in their midst and secure them somewhere until further notice. If they ask why—"

"Hold on. You can't be serious." Striding across the room, boots thundering, I stare down my eldest sister. "Your solution is to imprison us? The very people who were imprisoned for years—some for decades! What is wrong with you?"

Kalli's liquid silver eyes show no emotion. "We have no choice. We need to get a handle on the situation before it gets out of control."

"Guys?" Halira squeaks, but I can barely hear her over the frustration roaring between my ears.

"I can't believe you!" Before the monster inside me can break from its cage, I storm away. Some days I'm afraid of what he'll do if I ever let him back into the forefront. Dragging a tense hand through my tangled hair, I take a steadying breath.

"Look, there has to be another way. We should try talking to them."

"And we will," she assures me. "After we figure out what's happened with Qaeus. Halira? Did you send that message?"

Our youngest sister shakes her head.

"Thank you!" I say. "At least someone understands that we don't always have to rush to violence."

"It's not that." There's a quiver in Halira's voice that I'm only now able to hear. "I... I can't feel the wind. I can't feel anything."

Blinking, Kalli straightens. Her head tilts to listen to something that none of us can hear. If my own growing suspicions are any insight, she's searching for any whisper she can find of her own magic.

But the spark is gone. Not just weak or hiding, but completely torn from my being.

The only things I can hear are heartbeats.

"My magic is gone," Kalli says, too put-together for the level of chaos happening today.

"Mine too," Halira agrees.

We turn to the Elders who nod their confirmations of the same.

The magic that had once fueled this realm, the magic that the Primordials kept protected for generations and centuries, is gone. It died with Qaeus.

It's not long before we hear voices outside the tree, concerned druid citizens who are climbing the winding paths of the Eyve to seek an audience with their Elders. They come for comfort that no one can provide.

"Where are you going?" Halira calls to me as I make for the door.

"To see for myself."

Twenty or more people surround the tree already, with more piling up the paths. Over their thundering heartbeats, it's difficult to hear their cries, but I'm able to get the gist of it. They don't have magic either. No one does.

Despite magic failing, my thirst remains.

In defeat, and in a failed attempt to drown out the incessant *thump-thumping*, I cradle my head in my hands.

"What's going on?" the people demand.

Behind me, I barely make out Elder Henness' crackly voice. "I'm afraid we have tragic news to share. By now, I'm sure you've all felt it. Magic has failed, and with it, the Primordial Qaeus' life has ended."

If she meant to soothe anyone's worries, she does the opposite. Their hearts race and clamber. Their shouts grow louder. The collective fear and anger rises.

Elder Henness holds up her wrinkled hands. "We knew the day would come when the last Primordial would rest, but none of us expected our magic to go with her. We will be looking into it, promptly, and will keep everyone informed as we develop our understanding of the situation—"

"This is because of her!" someone growls from the crowd. It takes me a moment to realize he's pointing at Halira. "Everything was fine before she went meddling with the Heart."

Muscles flexing, Ryven steps between her and the crowd, shielding her behind him. "This had nothing to do with Halira! She corrected the balance of magic. Without her, the Primordial Qaeus would've destroyed all of Arcathain."

"But the Eyve would've been safe!" another onlooker bellows. "The Primordial and the demons weren't a threat to us."

I can do nothing but stare in astonishment. These people had lost loved ones to the demons. Maybe not as many as the Arcathainians, but enough that behemoths circled their borders at night and terrorized anyone caught wandering the Shadowthorn. Had they already forgotten that Halira had saved those poor souls too? People like me who otherwise would've been stuck inside demon flesh for who knows how long.

"They weren't natural!" Ryven argues. "Halira saved the Primordial—"

"And condemned us all!"

The change is palpable. The turn in the crowd like a living, writhing thing.

Ryven must sense it too, because almost absentmindedly his fingers weave through Halira's.

We have to get her out of here, I think, and almost the moment the thought crosses my mind, he glances my way.

Clear a path.

I'm not sure if he says it, or if I can just understand his meaning, but it doesn't matter. The crowd is just two outcries and a pitchfork away from becoming a mob, and the three of us need to be as far away from here as possible.

With no magic, and no real hold over these people, I use the only strategy I have.

Hissing, I flash my sharp fangs at the mob nearby. The people—hunters and bakers and blacksmiths and home-steaders—recoil away, their faces marred in terror.

I march forward until I'm standing beside Ryven. He nods, no words shared between us, but somehow both of us under-standing. We've been the monsters in these people's stories before. Why not do it again?

Together, we snarl, white fangs gleaming in the moonlight as we press through the crowd and clear a path. He tugs Halira behind us, too stunned to argue.

My other sister, however?

"Tor! Stop! What are you doing?"

I don't look back at her while I press on. I can't risk turning my menacing glare away from the people who I'm beginning to believe have wanted me dead from the moment I returned. All the time I agonized over my instincts, all the time I spent scoping out the surrounding towns and looking for a viable human so I wouldn't inadvertently feast among one of the hospitable druids here who had taken my family in, and for what? To be judged the moment something goes wrong?

And they haven't even heard about Heartkeep yet...

The moment they do, this place will stop being our home. If it ever even was.

"We're leaving. It's like you said, you need to get a handle on this before it gets out of control."

Only once the cries of the Eyve are long in our past, do the three of us take a break. We're only halfway down the treetop paths, but it feels safe enough since most of the town has migrated skyward, beseeching the Elders.

"What are we going to do?" Ryven huffs, his gaze trained on the path behind us.

I'm surprised Halira answers him so quickly. She hasn't said a word since we exited the tree. But maybe she's been developing a plan this whole time.

"We need to figure out what happened to the Primordial and what's going on with the blighted druids."

"*Formerly,*" I mutter.

"We have to prove our innocence."

The look Ryven and I exchange is one of guilt and shame. I think both of us already know that this isn't going to turn out well for us. I wish it didn't have to be true, but it is.

But maybe we can still help Halira, while some of our humanity remains.

"We should go to the other villages," I suggest. "Let's see if we can speak to the other formerly blighted druids. Learn all we can about the changes we've endured. Maybe there's something we're missing."

Halira nods. "Okay. I like that plan."

She starts heading down the path, but Ryven stops her. "Wait. It might be a while before we can return safely. We should gather some supplies, anything that we don't want to leave without." Something shifts behind his eyes, but I say nothing. "Meet at the border in two hours?"

Eagerly, Halira's head bobs. "Okay. I'll find Imryll. See if there's anything she can give us."

"Good. I'll head home and pack some gear, but I'll meet you at her place after." Ryven tucks a strand of hair behind Halira's ear. "Be careful."

She leans into his hand. "I'll be fine. Your homes are only a few yards away."

There's only sadness in his smile, but Halira doesn't seem to notice. She reaches up on tiptoes and kisses him before disappearing into the night.

"We're not leaving in a few hours, are we?" I ask him.

"No." He inhales a ragged breath, staring after the love of his life. "She's still recovering from everything we endured, from everything she sacrificed. Without her power now... I'm not ready to lose her."

"And with your desire to drink blood, it's not safe for her to be with us."

His eyes snag on mine, offense hardening his gaze, but it settles quickly. "You're right. She's not safe with me. Not until we figure out what's happening and how to stop it."

I keep my pessimism to myself. "Agreed. I owe Halira my life. I don't want to lead her into danger either. Are you ready to leave now then?"

The hesitation lasts a lifetime before Ryven finally sighs. "Let's go."

6

HALIRA

"Aunt Imryll! Are you home?" I stampede into her living area without invitation, and glance around for signs of her presence. When I don't see her in here, I make my way to the bedroom in the back. "It's a long story, but I have to leave. I was hoping you might have some supplies for the road?"

I open her bedroom door to find it empty. The rest of the house is still, and I'm forced to accept that my aunt isn't home and will be of no use to me. She's probably up top with the rest of the Eyve, wondering what kind of upside-down existence we've stumbled into.

Without my magic, I feel numb. There's no more electric pulse in my blood. No more vivacity in my surroundings. Everything is dull and dead.

I can't imagine how much harder it will be for anyone else who grew up here. I've only been using magic for a year or so. But druids have been using their magic their entire lives; it's as much a part of them as their skin or hair or eyes.

I can't think about them now though.

Those same people are the ones who were mere seconds away from demanding my head on a spike.

Racing back to the main room, I dig through Imryll's shelves. She might not be here to give me permission, but I think she'll be okay with me taking a few things to help us, just until we can procure our own. Salted jerky—of what animal, I haven't a clue, but it'll make for a fun guessing game. Dried fruit and seeds. A couple jars of pickled carrots and parsnips. I also make a quick stop back to her room to grab two extra pairs of socks—the last time I was stuck traversing the Shadowthorn my socks were barely more than tattered pieces of thread by the time I was done.

The satchel is the only thing I feel guilty about taking.

I've seen her use it plenty of times to gather herbs for medicinal use, to go to the market, or to pick fresh peaches from the orchard down below. She'll have to make do without it until I return.

Whenever that will be...

Without a glance back, I leave Imryll's home and walk next door. Since everyone is up at the Elders' home, and since I know Ryven is inside packing up as many supplies as he can find, I let myself in.

"Withering willows, Halira! You gave me quite the scare!"

My heart trills as well, completely caught off guard by the familiar, yet unexpected face I find sitting at the table.

"Jiordan, I'm so sorry. I didn't mean to just let myself in. I thought that—"

The middle-aged man chuckles, his sky-blue eyes alit with bemused confusion. "No need for apologies here. I've already told you. You're family now, girl. You're always welcomed here."

His immediate and full acceptance of me has meant more to Ryven and I than he knows. After losing my parents in a demon attack, I welcome the idea of finding my new family. At first, I thought it would be at the Castle of Nigh with my fellow Crusaders, but it wasn't until Ryven and I made it to the Eyve that I discovered my true home, and in it, new members of my family. It didn't matter that Jiordan's son, Ahl'Ro, Ryven's very own best friend, had been the one to kill my parents. We all lost someone that day. I lost my parents. He lost a son. Ryven lost a friend. There was nothing left for us to do but bond over the heartache.

I only hope our bond will remain strong. I won't be able to handle him turning on me like the rest of the Eyve. Their hateful faces still roar and scream in my mind's eye.

"Come in. Come in." He motions me over toward him. I enter, but I don't sit. My body refuses to be idle. "To what do I owe the pleasure?"

I blink away the memories and focus on what needs to be done.

"I'm here to meet Ryven. Did he not mention I was coming?"

Jiordan looks like he's trying to rack his brain and falling short. "He might've, but I can't remember. I'm afraid I haven't seen the boy in a couple of days, so if he told me a week ago, it's as good as gone. Benefits of aging."

"A couple of days?"

That can't be right. If he hasn't been here, then where has he been? And why?

Oblivious to the dire state of the realm, Jiordan laughs it off. "I swear, the two of you are getting busier by the day. It'll be good to see him though. You too, you know. It's been a while since we've all just caught up."

That's when what he's saying really sinks in.

Ryven hasn't been here in *days*. Which means he never stopped by.

But how is that possible? He was just behind me when him,

Tor, and I parted ways. Even if the boys chatted for a bit longer, he would've been here by now.

Unless something happened.

Jiordan is still smiling to himself, a mug of ale almost drained in his hand. "I know I'm not as great of company as Ry is, but you're more than welcome to stay here until he arrives. We could grab the ol' card deck—"

"I'm sorry, Jiordan." Wind whips at my heels as I pivot for the door, but I barely feel it. "I have to go."

"Wh-where are you going?" he asks, and as my hand twists the doorknob, concern hardens his tone. He stands, his chair scratching against the floor where he shoves it back. "Wait! What's wrong? Where is Ryven?"

Tears sting my wide eyes as I stare out into the night.

Jiordan has already endured the suffering of losing one son. He's already spent countless nights waiting up for someone who was never going to come back. I don't want to make him go through that same pain again, but there's too much to tell, and I don't know how much time I have.

If the druids got ahold of Ryven, they could be torturing him. They could beat him. They could imprison him, which would be worst of all.

"I—I—" Nothing I can say can alleviate Jiordan's worry or fear. So I settle for a small portion of the truth. "I don't know! But I have to go if I'm going to save him."

It's the best I can do before I bolt outside.

The winding, wooden paths that lead up the giant oak tree are nearly impossible to see at night without magic to light their way. Mostly, I rely on the moonlight. But anytime I run beneath a thick canopy, I'm blinded again.

I try not to think about falling.

The wind won't be able to save me.

I pass the place where the three of us stopped to develop a plan.

I pass people walking back down from the Elder's home, every one of them glaring—but thankfully not attacking. Whatever magic Kalli and the Elders mustered—and not real magic, considering that's still absent—must have worked. At least, for now.

But then, where is Ryven?

My Crusader tunic sticks to my skin from sweat by the time I reach the Elders' tree. I stumble through the doorway.

"Halira!" Kalli shrieks, racing to my side. She almost hugs me—almost. She might've if I didn't reek like our brother did after returning from a day in the fields back when he was a teenager.

My knees are weak. I haven't eaten all day, and though I used to be accustomed to such a diet when needed, my body is not currently tolerable of the endeavor. It's feeding two now, after all.

Practically crawling, I make my way to the couch and collapse.

"Where is Tor?" Kalli asks, her weight gentle as it settles on the cushion beside me. "Where's Ryven?"

They're the same questions I've been asking myself for the better part of an hour now, and yet it's only once she says them that I'm finally able to accept the truth. I think I've known it all along.

Exhausted and devastated, I finally lose it.

"They're gone," I croak, a sob and a wheeze battling for a place in my throat. My chest feels so tight, I can barely breathe. "They left."

"What do you mean they left?" Elder Henness towers behind us, peering down her gnarled nose like a hungry hawk. "They thought it wise to abandon their people at a time like this?"

Tutting, Elder Irene appears beside me with a kettle of

freshly brewed tea. "Stop that, Henness. It's not Halira's fault. Can't you see she's gone through enough?"

I can barely hear her, but I know it's impolite to refuse tea offered to you by an Elder, so numbly I take the cup.

Perched thoughtfully, Kalli's thumb rests on her bottom lip.

"For now, we let them go." I open my mouth to protest, or perhaps to call her out for being the heartless demon she is, when her silver eyes pierce mine. "I know you think I don't care, but I promise you I do. I care more than most. It's because I care that we have to let them do whatever it is that they're doing because we have bigger problems."

I know she's right, but the idea is unbearable to contemplate.

"You don't understand. He makes me whole, Kalli. We're a team. I can't just leave him—"

"You mean like he left you?"

Anything else I had planned on saying collides in the base of my throat.

"I don't say that to be hurtful, I'm just saying that he felt like he needed to go do something. I'm guessing it has to do with whatever changes he and Tor are going through, and we can't fault them for that. I'm sure they're scared. The way the people reacted earlier, it's no wonder they fled. But he and Tor will protect each other, and I know they'll return when they're ready."

"But—"

Looking exactly like our mother, she holds a hand up and I fall silent. "Halira, don't you see? That's all you have to hold onto right now. You have to believe they'll return because you have no other choice. They've given you none. They left—no one knows where. And short of going on a wild goose chase through the former Shadowthorn, pregnant and with a new unknown threat lurking about, you won't find them until they're ready."

Another sob wrenches from my heart, somehow more painful than the last.

There are times when I value my sister's wisdom greatly. Then there are times when I wish she would just let me wallow and make poor decisions. It isn't in her nature though. If she's thought through every angle of a situation and knows the best possible outcome, she's going to share her assessment. She's always been that way. And I suppose, though I'd rather lament a little longer, I should be grateful she's not allowing it.

"Until then," she says. "We occupy ourselves with an important task."

I set my teacup in its saucer and wipe my cheeks with the back of my hand. "Like what?

The corners of her mouth twitch with appreciation. "We were able to comfort the druids, but only with the promise of providing them answers."

"And where do we find those?" I ask dryly. "I can't communicate through the wind anymore. And visiting every village to gain and share intel would take weeks, if not months."

"That's why we're not going to all the villages. We're going to the only place I know that deals in more secrets, money, and information than a whorehouse."

"What do you—"

"Dearest sister, I think it's time we paid Cousin Alphonse a visit in the Capital. Don't you?"

7

TOR

Magic may have disappeared, but apparently some still remains.

It's not long after we leave the Eyve that Ryven and I discover we still possess some relic of power, though it is different from our druid abilities. For the first minute or so as we raced through the forest, worried that Halira might discover our plan and pursue us, our speed was heightened. Neither of us were sure how, and I seemed to last longer than Ryven, so there seems to be some sort of variation, but it's still curious, nonetheless.

"When was the last time you fed?" I ask him after a time.

We're far enough away from the Eyve now that I'm sure no one is following, and therefore we have no use of wandering silently in the dark. I've spent too many years wandering this forest without a companion. I refuse to do it again.

"Fed?" he asks, voice strained. "As in—"

"Yes. This is your nature now, or at least for a time. I suggest you start developing a tougher skin around your identity."

He clears his throat, considering. "You heard about Elder Nebadri's mouse? The one she found dead, killed by a cat?"

Glee overcomes me. I can't help it!

"You sneaky little bastard. That was you?" When he doesn't reply, I have to assume he's doing another one of his stoic expressions and I carry on. Until it occurs to me that we're talking about a tiny, disgusting *mouse*. "I'd hardly call that a feed. How much blood is even in those things? A drop?"

"It was enough," he grumbles, and I can hear how tight his jaw is clenched.

"Right. Yeah, I'm sure it was," I say, trying not to grimace and failing miserably. "I'm sure that's why you looked completely in control today any time Halira was cuddling up next to you. I'm sure you haven't spent the last few months wondering what my sister would taste like if you bit into her juicy throat and—"

"That's enough."

I scoff, fangs bared. "You're right, it is enough! Enough of you pretending that you're not starving and putting everyone else in danger. Or did you just think you could ignore it and it would go away?"

His silence is all the proof of his stupidity that I need.

"Wonderful. You've developed a fantastic coping mecha-nism." I roll my eyes and duck under a low branch. Just up ahead, I can barely make out a glowing aura that I have to assume is a village. Hopefully, if his sense of direction is accu-rate, it'll be the one we're looking for. "When we reach Hulbeck, remind me to find you something before you snap."

Still, Ryven doesn't speak.

I'm only mildly annoyed about it. Soon we'll be in Hulbeck, and I can find someone else to keep my company for the evening. The stories of my sister and what she did for this country have traveled far, and my white hair connects me directly to her. Everyone knows of Halira Devonshire, the Hero of Arcathain—or as they call it now, the United Realm—

and they're well aware of the sister and brother who aided in our small ways.

"Remind me again," he says after a while, all terse and agitated. "Why are we going to Hulbeck? There are a dozen towns between the Eyve and there where we could've stopped first."

"And risk running into them before we're ready?" When he seems confused, I elaborate. "Where do you think they'll look for us once they realize we've gone? You have thought about that, right? You know my sisters are quick, and fearless. And Kalli is in a position of power. They'll send scouts to all the nearby towns, searching for us. Unless you want to face them without the answers you're seeking, we can't be in any of the neighboring towns when they arrive."

He doesn't argue, and the rest of our walk to Hulbeck is in silence. Maybe it's for the best. We appear to be struggling to meet eye-to-eye on anything. The one thing we do have in common is we're all each other has.

Dawn is breaking, a creamy haze of violet cast over the horizon. It should be soothing. It should be awe-inspiring. But after spending years as a behemoth, the sight of sunrises still makes my heart rate spike. I remind myself that I'm no longer that monster, and trudge through the open gates, headed for the first tavern I see.

"Where are you going?" Ryven asks, his gravelly inflection scraping all the way down my spine.

I tense, slowly turning around to face him. "It's been a long night. I don't know about you, but I intend on resting, maybe getting some warm food in my belly, maybe sampling the local cuisine a bit—if you know what I mean—before we find the lord of the town and request an audience."

His grimace is answer enough.

Exasperated by his unwavering ethics, I'm seconds away

from throwing my hands in the air and being done with him, when a honeyed voice purrs behind me.

"No lord here, I'm afraid. But you're speaking to the lady."

A smile, handsome and cunning, washes away all of my previous frustrations.

"Even better," I say, extending my hand toward her. "I was just telling my friend here how eager I was to meet you."

"I'm sure." She watches me dubiously, but ultimately shakes my hand. "The name's Delilah Crowley, but Lady or Lady Crowley will suit."

I chuckle to myself, her blunt yet poised demeanor admirable.

Ryven pushes past me and bows so deeply his dark hair falls over his face. "I'm Ryven. Ryven Calligneous but, I promise you, you have no use of my surname. I'm from the Eyve where we hardly use them as titles."

"Ryven it is then." Respectfully, she dips her head. "And you are?"

My smile is unfaltering. "Tor Devonshire. Not originally from the Eyve, but I dwell there now."

"Devonshire?" she repeats, curiosity alit in her gaze. "As in related to Halira Devonshire, Hero of Arcathain?"

My grin deepens, cutting all the way up my face until I look like a jack-o'-lantern.

It works without fail. Every time.

Some men might be too proud to ride on the coattails of their sisters. But to that I say: have those men ever experienced fame by association and the untold benefits that accompany it? The free meals people are willing to serve me, the gallons of ale I've indulged upon at no cost, and the women.

Oh, the women.

They flock to me like moths drawn to flame, each of them desperate for one night where they forget their meaningless existences in exchange for a chance at tasting greatness. Even if it is by proxy. I might not have been the one to save Arcathain —piss on a mage, I'm fairly certain I was classified as one of the countries enemies at one point—but I'm Halira's brother and that's close enough.

"That's the one," I say, inching closer.

My next move is to suggest we go somewhere more private so I can tell her all about what it's like knowing Halira Devonshire.

But before I can, Ryven clears his throat. "We came because we'd like to speak to you about any...disturbances you or your people might've experienced lately."

"Disturbances? Such as...?"

"Such as certain kinds of attacks," I reply. "Not quite as ferocious as the ones we've seen from demons before, but..."

The thought trails off almost as soon as it begins when I realize she didn't blink when I mentioned demons. She hasn't even flinched. There isn't a single nervous twitch anywhere to be seen. And in my experience of ladies—whether they be nobility or not—they can't be within earshot of someone mentioning the wicked creatures without them going into hysterics.

Yet Delilah here doesn't so much as clutch at her breast or whimper.

"Ah, I see." Clasping my hands, I take a casual stride toward her. Now she wants to flinch. I can see it in the way her pulse is thudding on the side of her neck. But she remains strong, true to her nature. I take another step. And another. Until I'm close enough that when I lean down to speak to her my mouth brushes her ear. "You already know exactly what we're talking about. Don't you, darling?"

Without warning, something solid thuds into my chest and I'm flung backward. I crash into Ryven, the two of us falling into the dirt as Delilah dashes for us. She moves so quickly, she's no more than a blur.

Fangs bared, she stares me down, mere inches from my face. "Call me darling again and see what it will cost you."

"Forgive us!" Ryven growls, scuttling out from beneath me. His glare is molten metal stabbing into me, but he addresses the woman who seems to be more than human. "My friend and I have traveled a long way. We mean you no insult."

"Indeed, I meant the opposite of insult, my lady." Unable to stifle a bubble of laughter, I let it come madly as I push myself back to my feet and wipe away the dirt. "Especially if you're one of us. A—what do you call it? Calling ourselves new-demons or former-behemoths seems so unremarkable."

Delilah takes a cautious glance around, the streets beginning to fill with people ready to start their days.

"Not here," she tells us. Then with a flick of her delicate hand, she adds, "Follow me."

8

TOR

After the Lady Delilah grabs a thick, crimson coat and fastens the black buttons from her knees all the way to her neck, she tells a woman standing outside of the inn that she'll be back in time for tea. The woman offers to send us off with a pot, considering the chilly morning, but Delilah declines, and soon the three of us are walking upon a cave.

Ryven and I exchange a glance, though I'm not sure we're thinking the same thing. He looks like someone who thinks he's about to die, and I imagine I look like a young man who's just discovered his first brothel—I'm a little nervous, but that's part of the fun of stumbling upon a whole new world that you never knew existed.

"This used to be one of the salt mines," Delilah tells us. "But after my husband's tragic death here during one of his routine visits, I'm afraid I had to shut the place down. At least temporarily."

When she looks back over the black fur slung across her shoulders, the mischief reflected in her hickory eyes ignites my loins. As if she knows it, her devious gaze drifts downward before returning forward.

"This way," she says. "It's not much farther."

She's right, because after just a few more steps, she turns down one of the rocky hallways and leads us into a makeshift room of sorts. It looks like the place a foreman might've setup to go about their work on contracts while the real laborers hacked and chiseled away at the damp rocks down here.

At first, my eyes glaze over the scattered contents of the rickety desk. But then a glint of red catches their attention. A splattering of blood covers half of the discarded documents on the table. The ones that fell to the floor are in worse shape, the pages soaked through some time long ago, considering the edges that have already crusted and dried up in that rusty hue.

Striding into the room, she retrieves two apothecary tubes and jostles their contents before us.

"Here, drink these until we can find you both proper meals."

She tosses the tubes. Under most circumstances, I don't believe we would've had enough time to react naturally, but something primal in me awoke the minute we walked in here, and there was nothing that would've stopped me from snatching that vial out of the air.

With haste, I pop the cork off and dump the blood down my gullet.

Somehow, Ryven manages to refrain. "Where did you get this?"

Delilah's mouth twitches in amusement. "Ah, the senti-mental type? Good. You'll fit in well here. All of the blood I have on supply has been willingly given. And to your question earlier about less-than-ferocious attacks, there have only been five. The first was my husband. I tried to contain myself, for a time, but if you knew that man, you'd understand that the world is better off without him.

"There were a couple other deaths that followed shortly after. The similarities of the bite marks on the victims' necks—sometimes on their wrists or upper thighs—were of course too similar for me to assume I was an anomaly, although they didn't immediately lead me to my fellow noctis."

I arch an eyebrow. "*Noctis?*"

"You asked what we call ourselves. What better name to use than a reference to our nocturnal natures? I'm assuming, after all, that like me and the others, you were trapped in the Shadowthorn for a time, blighted and lost but not dead, despite your families who mourned you."

"You're a druid then?" Ryven asks.

Gracefully, she nods.

"*Others?*" I can't seem to move past that bit of information. My interest in Hulbeck and all that Delilah has to say is thoroughly piqued. Our visit is going better than I even dreamed possible. "Where are the others? Are they down here? In hiding?"

Her chuckle is light and airy. "None here are in hiding. We live our normal lives. It took some time and convincing—especially after the first ghouls were accidentally created—but once the people realized that we didn't want to hurt them, they were willing to cooperate."

"Cooperate."

I mutter the word as if it were a dream, and a rather obscure and unattainable one at that. I can't even fathom what it would take to earn the trust of the very people we need to feast upon for our survival. It would be like a wolf convincing a sheep to allow them to live together, among its children and brethren. Surely, it would only be a matter of time before the wolf's natural instincts kicked in and the sheep saw it for the predator it truly was.

As if she can read my thoughts, she continues.

"We've been able to foster a sort of peace between us and the humans. They understand our need for blood and provide it willingly. In doing so, we're kept satiated and don't have the need to hunt."

Ryven glances my way looking equally as bewildered as I am.

"I brought you two down here to make sure you were interested in doing the same."

Shadows flicker on the walls. Before I'm able to make sense of the situation, torches and bodies fill the cavern. Six in total. Some baring fangs, and others not, though I suspect they all possess them.

"What's the meaning of this?" I bellow, my Shadow Crusade training kicking into effect as I brandish my knife.

"I'm afraid I lied when I said they weren't down here. One of them saw us on our way out of town—you remember Miss Elizabeth? The one who offered us tea for the chilly morning?"

Sure enough, I turn around and realize I recognize one of the old hags—no teacups in sight this time, though.

Delilah continues. "However, I was being honest when I said I needed to be sure your intentions were pure before I allowed you to remain in my town for any duration. We've heard there are some noctis who refuse to feed unless it comes straight from the source. Of course, by now I'm sure you have learned that that's not possible without either killing someone or creating a ghoul, a fate worse than death for everyone.

"If you came here to feast upon my people and leave us in your heap of shit, then you may leave now with your life if you promise to never return. However, if you came seeking refuge, then we are willing to listen."

Ultimatums have never sat well with me, especially ones from strangers.

Who is she to dictate how we feed and upon whom? It's in

our nature now, I'm afraid. She's only postponing the inevitable.

But we came for answers, to find others like ourselves, and I'm not willing to relinquish that just yet.

Holding my knife up so that all can see it, I take a slow step backward until I bump into the table. I set the knife atop it, my hands hovering back into place overhead as I glare at Delilah. I should've known better, should've been able to smell this trap from a mile away, but I was too blinded by greed and lust to think clearly.

One of these days, maybe I'll learn my lesson.

Before I can think of a persuasive enough response, Ryven speaks up for the both of us. "Ironically, Lady Crowley, I believe we'll be of more help to you than either of us expected."

Skeptical glances dart around the damp cave, but Delilah keeps her sharp eyes focused. I'll admit that my intrigue is pulled just as taut as hers.

"How do you mean, exactly?" she asks, a hint of curiosity peeking through her tone.

Yes, Ryven, dear friend. How do you mean to rescue us from this dreadful situation?

"You say you've already established peace here, Lady Crowley?" he continues, confident, but not too pushy. "What if I told you the rest of the realm is soon going to need your expertise soon." When no one interjects, he pushes onward, and I'm fairly certain the plan is forming in his mind's eye as he says it aloud. "We just left the Eyve where the druids were moments away from setting the place on fire. And that was before they learned that monsters are in their midst again, only this time they don't wear the shadowy flesh of demons. Soon they'll be terrified and without a solution. They'll do what many have been known to do in the face of fear."

"They'll fight," Delilah answers.

Ryven merely nods. "Unless we can show them another way."

Following his thinking, and not wanting to be left out of the limelight, I pick up where he's left off. "The Magistrate of the United Realm is my cousin, you know. We could seek an audience with him, plead our case, show him that the noctis and humans can coexist without fear and death."

With a smirk, Delilah retrieves my knife from the table and hands it to me, handle first. "It seems you may have a point, Ryven. I think this is a partnership that has potential." She jerks her brunette head at the others, and they put down their weapons. "We will set you up in the inn—free of charge—so that you might rest and bathe before we convene to discuss logistics."

"Thank you." Ryven bows.

"It is nothing. We owe this to ourselves."

Extending an arm, Delilah gestures for the group to disband. We leave the same way we came in, though I'd be lying if I said I wasn't mildly disappointed that in all our time here next to the ocean, I never once saw one of the sirens Halira insists exist.

We're back in town soon though, and my aching legs are eager to find a bed for a few hours. Delilah leads us inside and makes sure we're checked in. The innkeeper retrieves clean linens and provides us our room numbers.

Ryven grabs his linens first and disappears behind his bedroom door without another word. The man shouldn't be moping; he should be happy! This was the best outcome we could've hoped for.

I reach for my piles of white sheets and a towel—

Delilah's soft fingers cup the tops of mine. "If you're not too exhausted after your bath, I encourage you to sample some of the local cuisine."

"Oh?" I ask, suddenly feeling like I could forego sleep for another week. "Do you recommend anything in particular?"

"Indeed, I do. Around lunchtime, she can be found in the big house on the hill on the western side of town. With no one else to dine with, she'll be rather ravenous."

With a crooked grin, I nod. "I'll be sure to bring my appetite."

KALLI

Before Halira joined the Shadow Crusade, and before I embraced my druid power, I had only made the journey from the Capital to Gravenburg a handful of times, and always in the company of colorful travelers who would spend their days sharing riveting tales of the complications of love, mishaps in their professions, drunken benders, and more.

The time went quickly, and quicker still once I started making the trip as my owl.

Now that I'm accustomed to the speed with which my white wings had been able to carry me, the journey to the Capital takes longer than I remember.

Halira's even more agitated by our slow advancement than I am, increasingly so with each new problem we encounter.

Over the course of our traveling, our carriage has to stop for two separate wheel repairs; one of the horses suffers an injury and we have to detour to the nearest town to procure a new one, only to find that the town is fresh out of horses, thanks to a recent wild animal attack that sounds oddly familiar to the incident in Heartkeep.

Our detour takes an extra week as we await our horse's recovery, but in the meantime, we busy ourselves with talking to the people.

Across the lands they're calling them *ghouls*, a horrifying byproduct of the bites inflicted by the formerly-blighted. Everyone is scared. Perhaps even more so than before. At least when it was just the demons we had to fear, we knew how to handle them: steer clear of the Shadowthorn, run from any shadowy creatures with claws and fangs the size of spearheads, and when in doubt, or when given no other option, use shadowsteel weapons if you've got them.

Ghouls might be easy to spot, but they're not sequestered to the Shadowthorn like the demons were.

More unsettling still, the formerly-blighted blend in with humankind almost effortlessly.

Until they smile.

We leave the humble village just as the fang-checks begin.

Who knows what they'll do to those found guilty of being formerly-blighted. One thing is for certain, this problem is quickly becoming global, and we can't speak with Alphonse soon enough.

By the time we reach the Capital, I've lost count of how many days we've been traveling, but it seems like well over a few weeks. Plenty of time for the formerly-blighted to have amassed the realm's fear.

As Halira and I walk the pristine streets of the Capital on our way to the Keep, we hear every rumor, every story gossiped in the crowded city. They tell stories of how one of the vile creatures ate all of his neighbors in the dead of night without a single person waking. They talk of some towns practically starving after the humanoid beasts devoured all of their livestock, not so much as leaving a single sow or heifer to be bred to rebuild the population. But worst of all, they lament over the swaths of ghouls ravishing towns and laying waste to entire communities.

"So much for our *united* nation," a woman hisses, fists shaking where they clutch the shawl around her shoulders.

"Yeah—" someone huffs a humorless laugh— "United in fear, more like."

Then our faces appear, three heads of iconic, white Devonshire hair coming into view. The silence that settles over the crowd isn't the peaceful kind of a quiet, drifting snow, but that of the quiet that befalls the mountain before an avalanche collapses it.

"Hey!" Someone shouts. "That's Halira Devonshire, the mighty *Hero* of Arcathain."

"Hero, my ass!" Another man plucks a ripe tomato from a food stand nearby.

He chucks it at us, the ripe thing smacking into Halira's shoulder.

Ire as dark as a moonless night flashes behind her grey eyes.

With a huff, she fills her lungs with air that she forgets is no longer imbued. I watch as the disappointment and worry settle into her features, making her look more like a frightened and lost child than the hero she is.

The people around us notice it too, for they brandish themselves with sinister grins as a barrage of vibrant colors is launched toward us.

I grab my youngest sister's elbow. "We have to go!"

Together, we race through the streets, drawing the attention of more onlookers if not from our hair alone, than easily by the angry mob chasing after us.

I throw my hood up to conceal what little of my identity that I can. Halira does the same. But with our hoods draped over our faces, we look even more the part of the villains they're making us out to be.

A young man dives for me from where he stood conversing

among friends. I'm tackled to the ground as one of his buddies does the same to Halira.

"Don't let them get away!" cry the people running up behind us.

"They have to pay for what they've done to us!"

When the young man pinning me to the ground pulls back my hood, he gasps. The pressure releases from where his knee had been on my back, but his hold on my wrists is still firm. I think he nudges the man atop Halira, because I hear him suck in a breath too.

"Look who it is."

"Well, I'll be as a pickled as a cucumber in vinegar. All three of 'em in one place?"

They help us to stand as the one holding me barks to the other, "Someone go get Alphonse. He needs to get out here before things get ugly."

Flummoxed, I jerk to get a better glimpse of my sister to find she looks just as surprised as I am. We're nowhere near the Keep yet and therefore nowhere near the nicer parts of the city. These sections are reserved more for commoners than men of Alphonse's status. In fact, I'm not sure his father, the former Magistrate Esmond, ever ventured to these parts.

When Alphonse vacates the tavern, however, I don't even care why he's here. I'm just grateful he is.

"Unhand them," he snaps, and his friends oblige. He turns his sharp nose toward the mob we've amassed. "All of you go back to your homes before you make fools of yourselves."

They don't budge until the friends in his company step forward, thick arms crossed, their menacing gazes daring the people for a fight. There are a few grumbles of nepotism, but eventually the people leave.

"What are you doing here?" Halira asks, rubbing her wrists.

He arches a slender brow and scoffs. "I could ask you the same. I wasn't expecting a visit."

I bristle. "We tried sending you a pigeon. Maybe it...maybe it didn't make it." If I had my crow, if we had our power, this wouldn't be a problem.

His expression turns somber. "You too then, huh?"

Our heads bob in confirmation.

"It's why we're here," I tell him.

"One of the reasons, anyway," Halira adds.

He plucks a flier from the wall behind us. On it is a horrific sketching of pale skin, sharp teeth, and glowing red eyes. He holds it up. "I can only guess the other."

"You grow wiser and wiser."

He smirks at Halira's compliment. "Come, let's continue this conversation with the Senate. They'll want to hear everything you have to say, and it'll save me time from having to parrot it back to them."

* * *

Being back inside the Senate chamber makes something ache deep inside me. I do my best not to let it show, but every now and then, I notice the look of pity Halira watches me with. She knows me better than most.

We wait in the back of the room until the Senate has assembled, some faces familiar to me, but others are new. After our uncle's corruption and Alphonse's ascension into leadership, he had to clean house to make sure only those with good intentions for the newly defined United Realms would remain on his advisory.

Then, there was my seat he had to fill.

I try not to stare daggers at the bloated man sitting in my chair—and try even harder to stop thinking of it as *my chair.*

Alphonse's wife, Fox, joins his side, and then we're ready to begin.

"Halira, Kalli," he addresses us. "Please, step forward and tell the Senate why you've come to the Capital today."

We've rehearsed this moment two dozen times. We've debated on which facts to share and which ones to withhold. Now that most of the realm knows about the formerly-blighted and the fall of the Primordial, there isn't much worth keeping secret, especially not if we want a viable solution for all.

We share what information we know about the formerly-blighted, about the ghouls, and about the fall of magic. We plead our case to the best of our abilities.

When we're finished, the bloated Senator stands. He speaks with the condescension of someone who is still trying to prove themselves in a world where they fear they don't belong. "We appreciate that you traveled all this way to share with us your experiences of the new threat we face, but I'm afraid none of this is news to us. We've been tracking the formerly-blighted for months now, and the attacks they've led across the realm."

Something in my mind snags on his choice of words.

The attacks they've led.

The way he speaks of it, he makes it sound like they're organizing with malignity, but we've seen no signs of that in our travels. Have they caused death and destruction? Yes. But the attacks almost always seem to be executed by one, not many. And as best as I can tell, they're committed in the name of hunger, not to smite the people or the realm.

"That's wonderful news," Halira says, bowing her head in a show of respect that I fear none of these people deserve yet. "Does that mean you have a plan in motion for getting these people the help they need?"

With the haughty nature of a teenage girl, the Senator folds his arms. He opens his mouth to speak, but Alphonse answers faster, something dark and somber weighing him down.

"We do, but I'm afraid you aren't going to like my answer."

Halira swallows. I can see her skin glistening with sweat. We're not just talking about the lives of innocents; we're talking about the man she loves. The father of her unborn child. We could be talking about her and her child as well— after all, who knows the lingering effects the Blight has on a druid.

"Well?" I stand taller, forcing my cousin to look me in the eyes even from halfway across the room. "Do you care to share with your neighbors your plan so that we might prepare for its unintended consequences?"

Fox squeezes his hand tighter, and he speaks, unwavering. "Currently? Without magic, we can't save them, and we can't risk having another demonic war on our hands so soon after the last. The people are scared and they need a chance to rebuild. To feel safe again."

Halira vibrates with rage. "Just spit it out, you coward."

He flinches, but sighs deeply. "Our only option is to kill them. The cleansing is beginning as we speak."

Someone tuts from the double doors behind us, making everyone in the room jump.

Tor's voice, rich and cloying rumbles throughout the chamber. "Do you really think so little of us, cousin?"

TOR

Every head in the room swivels to me and the noctis beside me.

What an intriguing sensation that overcomes me at having such command over a room, such power. It's no wonder our little cousin was such an insatiable, whiney brat growing up. He might not have held any real authority, but he witnessed it through his father, felt it by proxy any time they entered a room together.

This is the exact kind of influence and authority Delilah and I have been discussing over these past weeks. This is what our nation of noctis deserve. A seat at the table. A hand in the decisions being made about us for us.

And it would appear we've arrived just in time.

Extending my arm to the beautiful, dark-haired woman beside me, we step forward together. "I bring to you proof that we're not all as vicious as you make us out to seem."

"What is this!?" someone barks, slamming their fists on the table and rising.

"Who are these people?" another asks.

"They've come to overthrow the Magistrate!" bellows a third. "It's a mutiny!"

We anticipated this level of warmth from our welcome. In placation, I raise my hands. "Please, please, do remain calm. I can assure you this is no mutiny. No treasonous act. We've come merely to dissuade you from your decision to slaughter the noctis."

"The noctis?" My dear cousin looks genuinely perplexed.

As way of answering him, I give a lavish bow. While I'm hinged at the hip, I peek behind me to where Ryven fidgets nervously. I've asked him to remain quiet while we're here. We don't need him appealing to my sister, and then the Magistrate caving to her requests, and the Senate up in arms over their nepotism—yes, we've already heard the whispers leaking across the city.

If our people are going to plead their innocence and win their sovereignty, it'll need to be done fair and square. And that, after all, is the only reason we've come in the first place.

More and more noctis have flocked to us for shelter. For answers. We've done our best to help them all, but we can only assume for everyone who comes to us, there are a half dozen others who don't know about us or are prevented from reaching us.

Humans everywhere are turning on us. We're only safe together. We can only earn our freedom and continued safety if we remain a united front.

Ryven agreed, but every second that passes with us here, he looks more uncertain, and I fear he might not be as strong as he insisted.

Something pale and crumpled in his hand catches my eye as I stand, but there's no use dwelling on it now.

"Allow me to introduce to you Delilah Crowley of Hulbeck."

Taking her delicate hand into my own, I usher her before the Senate. She'd been a Lady for half a decade before her untimely encounter with a demon imprisoned her in the Shadowthorn, so she's still quite familiar with the customs of the court.

Delilah curtsies before them, a kind and inviting smile warming her features. She's usually so hard back home, I sometimes forget how gentle she can be.

"Magistrate," she says, voice pleasant, appeasing. "Senators."

"Lady Crowley," Alphonse replies, his nervous eyes shifting from the Senators to his wife. "We heard the terrible news about your late husband, Lord Crowley. My condolences."

"Thank you," she says, bowing again.

"Forgive me, but we requested a report from you regarding his passing, as well as any other unexpected deaths that might've occurred since the battle with the mages. We received no word from you."

A cool burst of panic flashes behind her eyes when she looks at me, but it's gone as quickly as it comes. We discussed this, as well. We knew they'd be displeased with her lack of cooperation and that it would only be a matter of time before they followed up with the people of Hulbeck to get the story.

Unfortunately, today is not the day to be admitting to the murder of one's own husband, nor is it the day to provide a detailed account of all of the deaths that have occurred over the past few months.

Today is about keeping them focused on our humanity, and Delilah knows this.

"My apologies, Magistrate," she says, long lashes fluttering. "We sent word almost immediately upon your request. To hear it did not reach you is extremely disconcerting. But we've heard that since magic fell that many of the courier pigeons have not been cooperating. If it would please you, before our departure, I would be more than willing to sit down with a scribe to provide you the information we have regarding those deaths, at least to the best of my memory. And when we return to Hulbeck, I'll send someone from town to deliver the rest to you personally."

While she speaks, I watch Alphonse, searching his expression for any clues as to what he might be thinking.

So far, all I find is doubt, amplified only by what one of his Senators shouts next.

"Lies!" The entire room shudders in the wake of the man's bellow. "My brother lived in Hulbeck when the Lord passed. He was one of the laborers you laid off after closing the salt mines. He saw you savagely murder your own husband in those caves. You didn't know he was there, but he was working late and saw everything. You're no respectable lady. You're a monster!"

Delilah tenses. This is an outcome we hadn't discussed, and I glare at her for not telling me there had been miners who fled the town.

Scrambling for words, I flail to save our position, to keep us focused on what really matters. "Alright, fine. Many of the noctis have stories of kills they regret. But Delilah is no monster."

"Delilah?" Kalli scoffs. "Is that why you've been missing for weeks? You've been off romping with a widower?"

I shoot her a glare that tells her to shut up, but fortunately I'm not the only one who feels that way.

Halira grabs her arm, jerks her back with a shush. "It doesn't matter where he's been. He's our brother." Then to Alphonse she adds, "He's family."

Just great…

"Family or not," I interject, struggling to keep hold of my impatience. "We are living beings who deserve a chance at life. We don't want to hurt you. We only want to live."

The Senator wields his finger like a crossbow at Delilah. "She murdered a man in cold blood!"

I can hold myself back no longer.

"The bastard had been raping her sister! While she was stuck in the nightmare of being trapped as a demon, he was visiting her younger sister every night and telling her she owed it to him because he was so in love with Delilah and missed her so much that it was the only way for his pain to end—the only way for him to be a good leader to his people. And every time that poor woman bore him a child, he had his best friend—the foreman who oversaw the operations of those salt mines where your brother was hiding like a coward—take the babe down into them and toss it into one of the endless pits."

"Piss on a mage," Alphonse says, rubbing his temples. "That's enough—"

"No, I'm afraid it isn't. You call us monsters but you're unwilling to see reason. You call us monsters when you employ and respect those far more monstrous than us."

There's no stopping my anger now. It rumbles beneath the surface like the churning waves of the sea on Hulbeck's coast, tainted with the vengeance of the innocent.

Since becoming *cured* in the most limited sense of the word, I've done nothing but try to contain myself. My urges. Other noctis have done the same. And for what? The people still hate us. Our leaders still want us dead.

"We came here today to prove to you that we are no monsters. That, despite our new nature, we've found a way to live in harmony with the humans of Hulbeck and to offer to help you teach the rest of the realm how to do the same. But you have no interest in hearing us, do you?"

Silence fills the room until I feel like I'm drowning in it.

Delilah inches closer, her slender fingers weaving into my own.

Behind me, I hear the crumpled piece of paper in Ryven's hand rustling in his nervous grasp.

But my eyes remain fixed on my cousin. On the shallow rise and fall of his chest. On his rapid pulse that's beating as swift as a hummingbird's flitting wings. He doesn't even have to respond. The answer is plain as the shadows etched in the dark grooves of his face.

"People have died," he says solemnly. "The survivors want justice."

A snap of his fingers brings the room into life. Soldiers—some of whom I think I recognize from my own training in Nigh—who had been lined up on the walls charge forward. Some of them lunge for the Magistrate, his Senators, and my sisters, shoving them back and out of harm's way, while the others charge toward us, their weapons readied.

"Go!" I shout, throwing my arm around Delilah.

Together we spin for the door. Guards close in all around us. They descend upon us, and we race for the door.

Out of the corner of my eye, I spy Ryven's frozen form, the pale ball of paper dropping from his grasp.

"Move!" I shout at him. "We have to—"

Delilah's weight intensifies in my grasp. She falls, and I nearly fall with her, but Ryven steadies me.

With mournful eyes, I glance at her still features. Her freckles already seem duller. Her luscious lips, dry. I register the sword pierced through her chest about a second before I see the guard behind her thrusting it out.

They want monsters?

I'll give them monsters.

Ryven tugs on my arm but I rip it free. Fangs bared, I lunge for the man who's just slain my woman. Flesh has never tasted so decadent, blood never so sweet, as that first bite of vengeance.

I suck as much of his life as I can manage, and then discard him. I chase after my fellow travelers, Delilah's people, watching in horror as soldiers continue killing them.

For every one they kill, I take another bite, leaving a river of humans in my wake who will soon turn into ghouls and wreak havoc upon the city. They'll have no choice but to kill their own. Or let them kill each other. I personally hope they choose the latter and I make a mental note to be sure to infect some humans in private before fleeing the city altogether.

"Let him go!" a deep voice growls in my ear. I peel myself away from the pathetic guard in my mouth long enough to register Ryven's brown, concerned eyes. "There's too many of them. Unless you want to die, we have to leave. Now!"

The laughter in my nose is bitter and hostile. The last thing I want is to die, to let them win.

As Ryven drags me out the room, guards descending upon us from every direction, but no longer daring to get close enough to be bitten, I scream across the chamber. "We tried doing it the right way! We didn't want to kill anyone. We just needed to survive. We weren't monsters, but we'll show you what monsters are truly capable of. Let the war begin!"

KALLI

"Let me go! Let me go!"

Only once the violence has come to an end do the guards finally heed my sister's request. The two guards holding her back step aside, and Halira stumbles forward.

"Halira, wait."

I call to her, but she doesn't listen. Perhaps she can't. The way she searches the Senator's chamber, screaming Ryven's name, fists clutched at her sides, I wouldn't be surprised if she couldn't hear much of anything but her own blood boiling in her ears.

I want to go after her, to try to comfort her in her time of need. But the past few weeks have only cemented the fact that I am of no use in that department.

Thankfully, Fox charges after her, a comforting word or two on her lips. With my sister tended to, I can focus on matters more suited to my strengths.

"What's wrong with you?" Eyes blazing, I whirl around on Alphonse. "They came peacefully!"

"We don't know that!" he protests. "Look, I know he is your

brother—he's my own cousin, too—but he showed up, uninvited and unannounced with a small legion of bloodsuckers at the ready."

"Yeah, ready to fight back if their lives were put under threat!"

Exasperated, he throws his arms in the air. "What's done is done. Now if you'll excuse me, I have to go figure out what to do with all of the victims he left behind."

As Alphonse reconvenes with his Senators for a quiet consultation, I take a look around the room. Bodies lay scattered across the marble floor. I wonder if blood has ever seeped on its surface. Unfortunately, I doubt it will be the last.

"I'm going after him," I hear Halira's quivering voice halfway across the room.

Fox rests her hand on her shoulder. "Are you really sure that's wise? I mean...he left. He could've stayed, but he chose to go. With them. Again."

With quaking fury, Halira finally implodes, a shriek piercing the mournful quiet that's settled over the room. She whips around, bolting for the door without another word. Fox chases after her. I might do the same if I thought it would do any good. She'll come back when she's ready.

As I take in the scene around me, I feel guilty for being so hard on my cousin. Heavy is the weight of the crown. Of all people, I should know that and be able to sympathize. A few short weeks ago, this could've been the state of the Eyve had I uttered the wrong word or made a slightly different choice.

People are unpredictable.

So are the noctis, it would seem.

Still, I can't help but feel certain that this is one mistake I wouldn't have made.

I walk throughout the room, aimless and only mildly aware of what the Senators are discussing behind my back. Tightening security. Hastening their cleansing sweep of the realm, beginning with Hulbeck.

As their conversation dies down, the Senators excused to the comfort of their rooms while Alphonse is to give the soldiers directives, some sort of parchment catches my eye by one of the columns. Right where Ryven had been standing.

I bend over to retrieve the crumpled piece of paper, unfold it, and begin to read.

Halira,

Hero of my Heart... You're so humble that you're rolling your eyes at that, just like you roll your eyes whenever someone calls you the Hero of Arcathain. But both titles are true though.

I wouldn't be here if it weren't for you. You saved my life. And if I know you at all, you're trying to save it again.

I don't want to be without you, but I'm lost. I fear I'm a danger to you and everyone we care about, but I don't belong with the noctis either. I feel adrift. I had hoped venturing out with your brother would help us find some answers, maybe even a cure, but none have been found. In fact, the way the others talk about it, it's as if they're content with this lifestyle—a nightmare I can't even fathom.

I heard that your sister smoothed things over with the druids and that you are no longer under threat. For that, I am grateful. But I worry the truce does not extend to me. If I am wrong, please let me know. I will return to you in a heartbeat. If you'll have me. The people here have discovered a way for us to curb our cravings without killing or creating more ghouls.

*I will keep my distance until I hear from you either way. I love you,
and I always will. You are a burning star in the dark,
never-ending sky.*

With love,
Ryven

"What's that?" Alphonse asks, making me jump and almost tear the letter in two.

"It's a letter," I say, turning around and handing it to him. "It's from Ryven."

He takes a few moments to read it.

I'm not sure what I'm about to say, but the following words bubble out of me. "Halira's pregnant."

Alphonse blinks, his mouth working around a slew of words, but he settles on, "This feels like the wrong time to congratulate her."

Absentmindedly, I nod. "Ryven doesn't know yet."

"I kind of assumed. If he did, I hardly think he'd let anything short of an apocalypse come between him, his woman, and his child."

"If she finds this letter..." I say, my mind churning with possibilities, with tough choices that will break her apart if she ever found out. She can't find out. "She'll tell him to return. But, Alphonse, I'm not sure it's safe for him. Not after this. Not anymore."

"What are you suggesting then? You know Halira. Once she finds him, she'll tell him to return anyway. With or without seeing this letter."

The answer has already presented itself to me, but I bide my time before replying, hoping some other option will present itself.

None come.

But I've made tougher sacrifices. I can survive a lie to my sister if it means saving her and hopefully the father of her child in the process.

"Then we'll just have to write a different one."

HALIRA

Months of carnage, months of trying to stop them and reason with them only to fall on deaf ears, have led us to this tragic moment.

Hundreds of noctis are gathered before the Keep, with Tor leading their ranks. He has hundreds of ghouls in cages, ready to be unleashed upon the humans when the battle begins. We have our own Crusaders and other guardsmen ready to battle the horde when they attack, but I can already see the bloodshed. I've witnessed battle before and seen the kind of destruction it can cause. The ghouls alone will be a formidable foe.

My newborn, Ursulette, coos in my ear where she sleeps. It's the most peaceful I've ever seen her. She's not been a very happy baby so far, and I can't help but wonder if she somehow knows that she's owed a father, or perhaps if she can sense the danger on our borders.

I watch from the tower, horrified and heartbroken as I gaze out at the army Tor has assembled.

This isn't the future I fought for.

We were meant to leave this darkness far behind. It was

meant to fade away in our history books as we rebuilt a better realm, one united for the common good of the people.

I never meant to unleash this greater, unhinged evil.

I never meant to lose my brother and Ryven in the process.

The letter he left me all those months ago rattles in my shaky grasp. I read it again for what must be the thousandth time:

Halira,

Hero of Arcathain, and Hero of my life. I wouldn't be here if it weren't for you. You saved my life when we were lost in the Shadowthorn. Now let me save yours.

Being a noctis is different than being blighted. I'm not even ashamed of the need to drink blood anymore. It's become a part of me, and I have to embrace it. Without magic, there will be no cure from this anyway. I have to live my life, and so do you.

You can't save me this time, Halira. And that's okay. You've already done more than enough for me.

I need you to let go of me now. I need you to move on with your life because I won't be the same person the next time our paths cross—I'm not even the same person now.

It'll be easier for the both of us this way.

With love,
Ryven

With the day finally upon us, I crumple the worn parchment in my fist and toss it from the window. I never believed this letter anyway. It never sounded like him. If anything, it sounded more like Tor trying to convince me to stay away, and so I'd done the opposite. I chased after them. For months. But I never found signs of Ryven anywhere, which only served to prove my point. He was never at the center of the carnage caused by the vengeful noctis because he hadn't embraced his bloodlust.

Whenever Ryven had left me in the past, he'd done so out of fear for what he might do to me, not because he was embracing his darkness. He'd never embrace his darkness.

Today I'd finally know the truth.

He'll be here today. He knows I'm here, and therefore he'll have to come to ensure that nothing harms me.

Here's to hoping I'm correct.

Adjusting Ursulette on my chest with one arm, I grab a needle-thin sword from the wall with my free hand. I've been instructed to remain here, where I'll be safe. But no one's safe here today. No one but me seems to realize how outnumbered we are, perhaps not in actual numbers for we seem to be evenly matched. But for every ghoul that barrels through our ranks, I suspect it'll weaken, if not immobilize and turn, at least three of our own.

The last place I need to be is in some tower, undefended by anyone but myself.

Ursy and I will be safest not quite in the heat of battle, but near it. Somewhere close enough that there will be other Crusaders, but not so close that we risk being surrounded and trapped inside the Keep that is about to fall.

And so, we head into the city.

Once Kalli left me in our room this morning, I began rubbing soot from the fireplace into my hair to disguise it. No one's the wiser as we descend the levels of the Keep, nor as we exit the building and make our way through the city, into the ranks. Sure, some heads turn toward us when they notice the babe asleep on my breast, but they're a bit preoccupied by the encroaching noctis to pay us too much mind.

Of course, the farther we stride into the soon-to-be-battleground, the less brave I become.

What if Ryven doesn't come?

What if I'm putting my child's and my own life at risk for a man who truly did mean what he wrote in that letter?

No. I can't let myself even think for a moment that that's true. Ryven loves me. I know he does. And I know the moment he sees his daughter he'll do everything in his power to protect us.

I just need to make sure we survive until then.

Easy enough for the Hero of Arcathain.

The war cries rise like a tidal wave crashing into the city. The wooden doors of the ghoul cages creak wide as they're released. The snarling that clambers from every street sends a skittering of fear up my spine.

I clutch my sword tighter and take one final look at my sleeping babe. So unbelievably precious and peaceful. At least she won't be awake for any of this. The healer assured me that the sleeping tincture will keep her asleep until sunrise tomorrow. I find little solace in knowing that if we do fall to the monsters, she won't feel a thing.

Down the road before us, I can start to make out the grey, frail shapes that bound up the corridor. They leap from the walls like spiders, venomous drool dribbling from their fangs as they growl and snap.

The Crusaders and guards beside me draw their weapons in unison. I ready mine as well, my Crusader training replaying in my mind.

Then the battle begins.

Swords hack through emaciated limbs. Fangs and claws tear through the leather armor and the torsos beneath. Blood sprays up Ursulette's back, and I want to stop. I want to turn around and run to make sure she's okay, to make sure that none of it got into her mouth or eyes. But I have to keep going. Keep hacking through the horde of ghouls—and the Crusaders who have been infected—or risk them overcoming us.

Dozens filter up the corridor like fog descending upon a glade. For every one I decapitate, another two fill its ranks. For every one I slay with my sword, another Crusader is butchered or turned in the process.

By the time forty or more of the arisen creatures are laying dead at our feet, and only two other Crusaders besides myself are standing, the noctis stride forth to finish the job. My heart leaps into my throat as I peer among them, frantically searching for the dark hair and russet eyes that I've missed so much over these past few months.

Instead, I find the opposite.

A pair of arctic eyes framed in snow-white hair steps forward. Tor almost looks amused to see me, until his gaze wanders down to my daughter. On instinct, I press her closer, and I know then that I would even kill my own brother to protect her.

"Well, well. What a surprise," he says, holding up a hand to his fellow noctis.

All stop but two, who lunge forward at his command with the swiftness of the wind and tear out the throats of the Crusaders beside me. They fall to the ground and the rest of the noctis descend upon them. Terrified, I scuttle away, my back slamming into a wall.

Tor is beside me just as swiftly. He runs a long, sharp nail through Ursulette's fine hair. "What an interesting turn of events."

I jerk her away, sliding down the wall and putting enough

distance between us so that my sword can keep him at bay. "Where is Ryven?"

Arms up, he backs away. "You know that bleeding heart. You really think he'd come here? To a battle where he knows his friends and family will be slaughtered? Please. He's been beside himself, truly. The epitome of despair and self-loathing. But he's been given no other choice but to align himself with me now, has he?"

"He belongs here. With me. With his family!"

With a tilt of his head, Tor feigns consideration. "Or, perhaps he's building a new family amongst people who accept him for who he is."

"I do accept him!" I bellow, feeling like Ryven is yet again slipping through my fingertips. They both are, but at least with Tor I knew he was gone. But Ryven? How could he not come? How could he let this attack happen and not be here to stop it? Is he so far gone already that he no longer cares about my well-being? Maybe his letter was more genuine than I gave it credit for...

"Halira," Tor says sweetly, almost mentor-like, and I can almost remember our childhood together. The way he'd look out for me. The way he'd share all the hard lessons he'd learned about growing up in the rough Wallows. For half a second, I see my big brother, and think maybe there is still a way to save them. To save them all. There has to be. "Halira, you don't accept him. You want to change him, just like the others do."

Embarrassment washes over me at how right he is. Even now, it was exactly what I was thinking.

But he can't want this. He can't want to drink blood, I'm sure of it.

"We are who we are," he says with finality. Then, like a viper poised to strike, he trains his sights on my daughter. "Now, tell me more about this bundle of joy you've got there. I take it she's his?"

I hug her tight, wishing I could somehow shove her back into my body through my skin. I'd wanted to hold on longer. I wanted to wait to deliver her until after the war. But she'd been ready. Early, even. Part of me thinks she wanted to be here as much as I did, perhaps foolishly believing it would be her chance to meet her father.

"Does he know?" Tor asks, but then laughs to himself before I can answer. "Never mind. Of course he doesn't. He wouldn't have stopped talking about her if he had. But let me ask you this, dear sister. How *is* she?"

The question catches me so completely off guard that I struggle to respond. "Sh-she's fine. What do you mean?"

"Does she cry?" he elaborates. "Does she never seem satiated after her feeds?"

My spine becomes solid ice.

There's no way he could know that, so few people do. Only Kalli and Fox, and I suppose Alphonse if I know anything about Fox's inclination to share with him all of her secrets.

I've been consulting midwives, healers, I even hired a wet nurse to see if maybe it was just my milk Ursulette wasn't taking to. None of the methods we tried work. Although she will suckle, she is uninterested in milk.

Only when I've pricked my finger and let the drops fall on her tongue has she been contented. But certainly, Tor would have no way of knowing any of it.

My silence summons his repulsive grin. "Her teeth haven't come in yet, but what happens when they do? What happens when the people see her fangs and recognize her as the monster they've come to fear? How will you protect her from the entire realm?"

I—I can't answer him.

I've worried the same thing ever since she was born.

Without my magic, how will I protect her? It seems an

impossible enough feat to protect her from the ever-growing ghoul population, but from humans and monsters alike?

I am but one person.

Our eyes locked in some kind of prison of sympathy, Tor extends his arms out to me. "Give her to me. I'll take her to Ryven. He'll be a good father, Halira. He'll care for her and perhaps find some ounce of love in this world again."

"No." My lip trembles, all of my fears crashing down around me. "She's all I've got."

"She can't stay here. Not safely."

"There can be peace!" I yell. My heart wants to shatter but Ursulette's warmth is the only thing keeping it in place. "We don't need to go to war! Call off your army and talk to Alphonse!"

"I tried that!" he bellows back at me, pain sinking into the depths of his eyes. "Remember? And instead, he killed the woman I loved. He would've killed us all if we hadn't managed to break away. He would've killed Ryven."

"No." I shake my head adamantly. "He wouldn't have."

"He would've, Halira. The orders he's given his guards to tear the realm apart on a fang-hunt? Tell me, did he say to spare anyone? Did he say, *oh, and if you find my cousin's lover, please return him so that they may live happily ever after?*" He doesn't let me answer. He doesn't need to. We both know the truth of what he's saying. "No, he didn't. We came for peace, and he opted for war. Not the noctis."

I'm not sure I know when I did it, but at some point I drop my sword because my hand is now caressing the back of Ursulette's head. I don't want to admit what I already know subconsciously—that this is goodbye.

"When will it end, Tor?" I ask my big brother. "Unless someone stands up and decides to be the bigger person, it will just go on and on. But you can be the bigger person. You can end this now!"

With profound sadness, he shakes his head. "Unfortunately, I cannot. There is no going back now. Alphonse has a country he's trying to protect and a decision he's made. I have my own people who look up to me, people I have to protect."

"And what about me, Tor? What about your sisters?" The hot tears stream down my face like iron pokers taken from the fire. "Don't do this."

"What's her name?" he asks me, and it takes me a moment to register who he's talking about. "May I please know the name of my first and only niece?"

I sniffle. "Ursulette."

"Beautiful." A ghost of a smile whispers across his features. "I'm sure Ryven will agree. And I promise she will be well cared for, as long as you and the Shadow Crusade stay far, far away from Neveridge." At my curious gaze, he adds, "The mages former territory."

I'd heard the noctis had to flee Hulbeck after Alphonse sent his guards there, but I didn't know where.

If Kalli were here, she'd tell me it is the only way. And somewhere beyond my tangle of panic and heartache, I know they're both right. But I can't let her go. I can't willingly give my only daughter over to a man who I'm not even sure I recognize anymore.

"I can't give her to you," I tell him, a bit sorrowful. "I'm sorry. I know what you're saying is true, but...I'll figure it out. It's me and her now."

Tor moves so quickly I don't even notice he's gone from where he was standing a healthy, safe distance away, until I feel his presence beside me where I'd been sliding down the wall.

Something pinches my neck.

Fangs? I'm not sure.

But my vision clouds, and my knees feel weak.

The words drag on my tongue like drunken things. "What did you do...?"

"Shh," Tor whispers into my ear, catching my elbows and easing me down. "Rest. This is for the best, little sister. Your daughter needs to grow up around her own kind where she will be loved, not feared."

As darkness encroaches, I strain to hold onto the light.

But as it turns out, I have none left.

When I awaken, hours—perhaps days—later, the battle is over. The moans of the dying that surround me make me wonder if I'm not dead too, for the hole in my chest sure feels life-ending.

As I stumble through the Capital of rubble, only one thought fuels my weakened steps:

I will find my daughter. I will get her back.

Thank you for reading *Hunger & Cursed Shadows*!

To be continued in
Blood & Magic Eternal

PREORDER NOW!

Leave a Review

Help other readers find this dark saga by leaving a review on Amazon, Goodreads, Bookbub, or any other reading website. Even a simple "I loved it!" can really help!

ARC Team
If you're someone who loves leaving reviews and you're excited by the idea of having early access to all of my books, check out my website for more information on how to join my ARC Team: www.jessacawillis.com/ARC

Social Media
And last but not least, if you'd like to stay connected, you can find my social media links here: https://linktr.ee/jessaca_with_an_a

PRIMORDIALS OF SHADOWTHORN
Epic Dark Fantasy Romance

Ruled by tyrants. Hunted by demons.
This vengeful huntress is ready to fight back.

When Halira's parents are slaughtered by the horrifying demons that plague her lands, she joins the Shadow Crusade, a legion of warriors determined to slay the last living Primordial, end its reign of darkness, and destroy demon-kind once and for all.

But as her training begins, Halira soon discovers a secret about the forgotten magic that once thrived throughout the lands, one that could threaten her very survival.

Will Halira be the savior her country needs, or will her own dark secret force her to hide in the shadows?

~Check out the Primordials of Shadowthorn series on Amazon~

REAPERS OF VELTUUR
YA Epic Dark Fantasy

*In a realm where murderers are taken by
the Councilspirits and forced into becoming Reapers,
one girl is on a path to redemption...*

Sinisa is a Reaper of Veltuur, an assassin born from the underrealm, with fatal magic coursing through their veins.

For three years, she's slain her targets dutifully. Now she just needs one more kill to ascend as a Shade, a coveted status of power. And when the King of Oakfall requests a Reaper to execute his daughter for an unforgivable crime, Sinisa is first to volunteer for the job.

It *should* be easy.

But when the Prince discovers his sister is in danger, he flees the palace with her, leaving Sinisa with only two options: journey through the mortal realm to find and slay her mark, or face the consequences of returning to the underrealm empty-handed.

It's no choice at all. She has come too far to stop now.

Besides, no one can outrun a Reaper… Or can they?

~Check out the Reapers of Veltuur Trilogy on Amazon~

Supernatural powers destroyed the world...
Now four unlikely heroes have to save it.

The world ended two years ago. They called it the Awakening: the supernatural event that gave some people powers and left others normal. Nations went to war and millions died.

Sean was one of the first to Awaken, but it wasn't until he walked in on his brother's brutal murder that he learned of the darker nature of his power: blood calls to him, and he to it. And in that moment, he showed his brother's murderers no mercy.

Now Sean must fight to keep his inner demons in check, and his path to redemption begins with the establishment of a sanctuary for people like him, people with powers: the Awakened.

But not even in the apocalypse are the Awakened safe...

Can Sean and three strangers unite the remnants of mankind when everything else has fallen apart? Can they face the darkest horror this new world has yet to offer?

~Check out The Awakened Quadrilogy on Amazon~

ABOUT THE AUTHOR

Jessaca is a fantasy writer with an inclination toward the dark, epic, and adventure sub-genres. She draws inspiration from books like the Nevernight Chronicles & ACOTAR, videogames like Dark Souls III, and television shows like Game of Thrones and The Chilling Adventures of Sabrina. She is a self-proclaimed nerd who loves cosplay, video games, and comics, and if you live in the PNW, you just might see her at one of the local comic conventions in one of her favorite RWBY cosplays!

www.ingramcontent.com/pod-product-compliance
Lightning Source LLC
Chambersburg PA
CBHW071816190726
48292CB00008B/2863